The Greed Gene

The Greed Gene

Angus Wynn

Writer's Showcase
presented by *Writer's Digest*
San Jose New York Lincoln Shanghai

The Greed Gene
All Rights Reserved © 2000 by Angus Wynn

No part of this book may be reproduced or transmitted in any form or by any means, graphic, electronic, or mechanical, including photocopying, recording, taping, or by any information storage retrieval system, without the permission in writing from the publisher.

Writer's Showcase
presented by *Writer's Digest*
an imprint of iUniverse.com, Inc.

For information address:
iUniverse.com, Inc.
5220 S 16th, Ste. 200
Lincoln, NE 68512
www.iuniverse.com

This is a work of fiction. Incidents, places, characters, names, and plot are the product of the author's imagination or are used fictitiously. Any resemblance to actual persons, events, establishments, or locales is entirely coincidental.

ISBN: 0-595-12966-8

Printed in the United States of America

With thanks to Angus, Eileen, Judi, Ed, Jerry, and Blaine.

Chapter 1

Room temperature. A constant seventy-five degrees F. He guessed that his persistent exposure was giving him a room temperature IQ or the other way around—he had to have a room temperature IQ to live under these conditions for so much of his life, doing what he was doing, for so much of his life. So much for his life.

Fluorescent lights. Were they full-spectrum? He'd never asked. When he got the job three years ago, Ben Kramer hadn't asked much. Two weeks vacation and eighty grand a year. Heaven. With fluorescent lights and room temperature. Ben didn't know anyone who'd know about the lights anyway. Most Americans lived this way he supposed, so how much harm could it do?

How was nature selecting among the genes of these modern workers, who were living under such predictable circumstances for major portions of their lives? How were we evolving? Some sort of tolerance genes were being chosen, Ben thought; genes that conferred resistance to the constant pounding of banality—non-thrill-seeker genes, boredom-suppresser genes, or whatever genes.

"Taking a breather there, Ben?" blurted Eugene Richmond, his section head in the pharmaceutical division of Tailored Genetics—just another of the several well-established, hot biotech firms that had been around for the past five years at least.

"Yeah, Gene, resting my wrist," Ben replied, heart still beating overtime. Gene had scared the hell out of him, again. Whereas many researchers chose to play music while they worked, Ben preferred quiet; Eugene kept his personal volume too high.

"Maybe you should go see a physical therapist for that wrist; insurance'll pay for it. We've got a deadline on this project, Ben. We've got to get moving on this—get her wrapped up. Company needs those government contracts to keep flowing our way. Can't let a little micropipetting get in the way of progress."

"Yes, Gene, you're right. I'll get some ultrasound or pills or something."

"Good, Ben, sounds good. Keep up the good work," said Eugene, as he left the lab, headed undoubtedly to the adjacent one for another check.

Project was the nice word for it. Assignment was what it was. A full-grown scientist and Ben was still being told what to do. This one involved a contract with the Federal government—Justice Department. Overcrowding in prisons had become a serious problem—one that even politics could not solve—so some pol on some committee, somewhere, had come up with a brilliant idea. It's all relative, really—the brilliant bit—but for a career politician or any government employee, for that matter, any idea that did not involve shifting or disguising funds was a brilliant idea. Genius! This particular conception went as follows: prisons cost money; number of prisoners increasing; need for more space to house criminals…solution? Build more prisons—no money, not in my backyard, other forms of crime deterrence needed. No, find a way to house prisoners in less space—economize on space; pack 'em in better! How could we? It'd be inhuman! Solution: make it less inhuman. How? Genes—they're doing wonders with genes. Do it with genes.

This was about as far as this stellar notion had been articulated by these government officials. This committee (Committee A) contacted other appropriate committees (B-F) and it was decided that no time should be wasted. A letter announcing this research opportunity was formulated by Committee A and—after lengthy modification and final approval by all relevant committees (F,C,D,B,E—in that order)—the announcement was announced to the public, sent to the big biotech firms, placed in magazines that geneticists would be expected to peruse, and mailed to universities and colleges. Ads were placed in major newspapers and the announcement was otherwise distributed before the public—in as fair a manner as possible—so that all interested parties would have a fair chance at submitting a research proposal for doing something wonderful with genes to provide for the packing of prisoners in prisons more efficiently.

Proposals poured in, and not merely from informed or misinformed geneticists. Tailored Genetics was in the pipeline—got the news early—and Ben had been instructed to draft the proposal. And he won the money. His job was going good.

As it had been since he'd been hired. Lots of work came his way, as it was supposed to. Not much of it—well, none of it really—of his own choosing, but what was the difference anyway. He'd get the samples, micropipette using the Pipetman (otherwise known as "load the gels"), run 'em, transfer them to nylon membrane probe blots, wash the filters, and expose them in a phosphorescent imager. Waalah! Results! Another day, another gel.

Not much of a social life for him waiting at the end of his daily commute back north to Ventura. Not much opportunity to meet any woman, anywhere. There weren't any to speak of looming around the halls at work and he really didn't get out much back home. Nice apartment, great furniture, lots of money, stereo, tasteful music, he could cook—had all of the necessary resources. At five foot ten, maybe he simply wasn't tall enough. Ben suspected that this was not the reason for his solitude; the reason was that he was not motivated. He lacked the drive. It was a control issue—he had no control over his life! He was merely another cog in one big manufacturing machine, self-esteem on hold, perhaps indefinitely.

Another re-run of Ben's internal monologue as he slowly cruised, or belly-crawled, through the Friday evening commute home. Pull into the parking lot, get out of the car, check the mailbox—I've got to meet some people who lead normal lives, he thought, people who could show me some fun. Up the stairs, and hey, here's my pad. The cool bachelor back at his casa. Friday night, watch out world, TV'll be burnin' tonight! Unlock the front door...maybe if I write a very creative personal ad.

His Friday night routine was shattered by the ear-splitting blink of his silent answering machine; he had a message! Machine really did work. He pressed the play button.

"Hey, Ben, it's Ashley. You surprised? Listen, I'm in Santa Barbara today at a meeting, and since I'm already up here and it's been almost a year, I thought we could get together for dinner and catch up tonight, if you're free. So, I'll be by your place at around seven and if you're there, you're there. Sound okay? Anyway, see ya."

If she could only see what I truly am, Ben wished. Oh well, it'll be pleasant to see an old friend anyway. It'll get me out of the house, circulating, continued his thoughts with one sly, shit-eating grin.

Tonight the women of Ventura will see Ben Kramer escorting a very attractive woman. Man about town. Man about town? Where the hell did that come from? Hunk? Nope, didn't meet the six foot minimum standard. And you also don't get there with this kind of talk, even if it is to yourself. Must talk more laid back, contemporary. And right now...man!

Ashley Bradford was a bright, redhead. Very bright and very red—skin only lightly freckled. Ben was forever in awe over the fact that she never indicated any attraction toward him. Or he was awestruck at his inability to sense the incredibly obvious sexual signals that she'd been broadcasting his direction over the years. In either case, she had him nonplused. He had rid himself of the necessity to imagine her as a male, tobacco-chewing, construction worker, who practiced—but had never perfected—poor hygiene. No, she'd been upgraded to either a sister or lesbian. In any case, he could handle it without too much discomfort; she was one damn beautiful lesbian!

They proceeded to the Sundown, a bistro/bar on the beach, so you could actually watch the sun deposit itself; very popular among the young, single professionals of Ventura. You could be fairly certain that any of the patrons that you encountered at the Sundown was, in fact, a resident of Ventura. Not many Out-of-Towners tended to venture there for nightlife—didn't know what they were missing, or they did.

"That's bathetic!" Ashley declared, as she set down her glass of Mai Tai.

"What's bathetic? And what is bathetic? What does bathetic mean? Needs a bath?" Ben wasn't in the mood for a vocabulary lesson.

"Your entire approach toward the opposite sex," she replied, the dim lighting of the Sundown and the liquor-dulled edge of Ben's vision prevented him from witnessing her expression—intense: lots bulging, unhappy neurons somewhere in there.

"Needs a bath?"

"No, it's bathetic; consumed with bathos. Pathetic."

"Well, why not say pathetic then? Save us some air. I'm not the English major; can't engage in any vocabulary joust with you, I'm unarmed! Anyway, what is so pathetic—or *bathetic*—about my attitude towards women?"

"Not really your attitude, more your approach, I'd say. You're not going to meet one who shares your interests, opinions, desires…in a bar. The only guarantee you have there is that you both like alcohol, the foundation of every solid relationship."

"Well, thank you damned much, your lawyership. So what do you suggest?"

"There must be some single women at your job. If not, try taking some adult classes. You could figure this out, you're not stupid."

"Thanks for the compliment. And, you're right, maybe I'm just wallowing in self-pity. Maybe I'm too tired to get motivated. What about you? Why aren't you hooked up with someone at the moment?"

"No time. Same reasons." She was already feeling very disturbed with herself at having even brought up the opposite sex subject. Vulgar phrases, such as, "How's your love life?" should carry a sentence of two years—no possibility of parole.

Sensing that Ashley was about as enthusiastic with their current topic of gab as he was, Ben pushed the yellow alert, "Big picture, it's all too common these days. Fifty percent divorce rate, growing gap between the rich and poor, gun control, video games, etc., etc."

"Ain't it the truth. Wow, you've got a way of distilling everything down to the vapor it deserves. Why haven't I got a mate? Answer: too many handguns out there, and hey, those damned kids are playing too many video games!"

Ben smiled, "Other people seem to be getting coupled," and immediately regretted having resurrected the subject. Don't kick the sleeping dog, the damned thing will get up and crap on the sofa in the living room; cough up on one of those doilies Mom crocheted, and start barking at something no one sees, forever.

"Hey, dammit, haven't we got something else to talk about?" she demanded, as her fist met table with a woof!

This racket got the attention of some Sundowners at nearby tables. Ben glanced back at a few with one of those, "What got into her?" looks before he said, loudly, "Dammit, you're right Ashley!" And emphasized this with a bit of furniture, as well. If that pine could talk.

They both grinned at each other, this brief public display, turning their heads slightly to each side to assure themselves that they were not still on stage. Having regained anonymity, they resumed.

"Seen anyone we know lately, Ben?" asked Ashley, as she downed the remaining half of her drink and reached for the pitcher for a refueling.

"The old gang. Nope. Haven't seen a familiar face since last Christmas, when I went back up north to see my folks," he replied, polishing off his glass and reaching for more Mai Tai.

Ashley was attractive when they met at seven, but now she appeared almost irresistible—three Mai Tai magnificent! Control, Ben boy, keep it down. Down, boy!

"Well, I've got some friends in L.A. Not close, but sufficiently entertaining. It would be nice to see some of the Berkeley crowd again, wouldn't it?"

And so the Petri dish was inoculated, thought Ben two weeks later, as he was beginning to pack for his weekend trip up to the Bay Area—the re-union of his own small band of former Berkeley University Co-op dwelling, outlaw wannabes. A group that hadn't been crazy enough to drop out to play Bridge almost non-stop or cope with classes by chemical means or become obsessed with politics, but one that, at least, avoided the Greek system and the dorms. Caught in the middle-left, as it were.

Slow cadence of drumbeat from the desert's horizon, increasing in volume and tempo; a blast of horns ending on a high pitch, the drumming stops…and then came five.

Chapter 2

BIG 'N HARD (BNH) was an outrageous name for a computer chip company, but so was the President and CEO, Gil Bateson—outrageous, that is. He founded the firm before graduating from San Pedro Institute of Technology—he dropped out. Gil was a chip-designing prodigy. Chips in his veins. Specialized in designer chips when he was a kid. Smaller, faster, cheaper—hardware was his business; circuitry, his art; competition, his life! Yes, the man was highly competitive. Even though he possessed little to no business savvy, Gil succeeded—Bateson got ahead. He beat, bruised, crushed, coerced, smeared, smashed, jerked, juiced, ground, grinched—he generally out-bizzed his competitors. Again, not because he possessed any business acumen whatsoever, to speak of, but simply because he surrounded himself with the best, the most ruthless, the nastiest men and women of commerce that he could buy. And he'd memorized all the right business slang, so at least he had some idea what they were talking about. And his accountant, brother-in-law—whipped as he was by Bateson's sister, Bernice, could always be counted on to keep the books in order. Gil was in the chips, as long as the market didn't move to another corner.

Rent was cheaper up north, so he moved the operation up there in the late 80's. The Seattle area seemed to be one of the burgeoning centers for high-tech and the town of Renton was close enough, so Big 'N Hard found its home there, next to Boeing. It seemed fitting, since

Boeing's products also happened to be big and hard. Gil would often ride on one of their big and hard products—off to some conference—thinking about profit margin and the bottom line.

Gone were the days when Gil could rely solely upon his fleet of talented, expensive computer designers to keep the firm ahead. Those engineers that once commanded six figure salaries, with a house thrown in as a signing bonus, just weren't needed as much anymore. The software boys had beat them at the hardware game—they had computers designing computers! All that was left for the hardware jocks to do was punch a few keys and occasionally come up with something novel that wasn't in the program. The boys of hardware were getting pushed out of the game; demand for software scribes would soon go limp as well, but they hadn't yet seen that coming. Innovation was a smaller part of the show for BNH; stripping other companies of their product had become more the rule.

Bateson kept the edge of BNH honed by strategizing with select senior staff—usually once a month—in what he called Core Group Meetings. Gil would meet with four Senior Vice Presidents: the CFO, the Director of Sales and Marketing, the Director of Corporate Business Development, and the General Manager, Technology and Manufacturing Group. The Boys plus Susan—who was one of the Boys, anyway—The Think Tank, A-Team, First String. They knocked heads, or rather, Gill knocked on their heads and they answered. The Boys knew the answers, that's why they had made the Team. Most of the decision making had already been done by e-memo between the Chief and a particular Core Group member (CC'd to the rest of the Tank), but the meetings were still essential. Aside from all the back-slapping, fun-poking, and rallying of pep, this conference allowed Bateson to touch base, arrive at consensus, and promote his "stomp-the-bystanders" approach to the market. Every Core Group Meeting began with the same gospel.

"What are we?" Gil asked, as he always did, loudly.

"Big 'N Hard!" all replied in unison, also loudly. This was followed by an earnest applause that they always felt they deserved.

"Good afternoon, folks, guess it's that time again, right? Well, let's get down to it, I know some of us have some work to do. So, let's start with say, Bob. Bob, what's up?" Bateson inquired, seating himself at the head of the table in the boardroom.

"Well, we're looking pretty good. Got reasonable, positive cash flow, inventories and accounts receivable aren't up much over last year's, and, gentlemen, sales are up 120 percent," Bob Pridgeon stated, taking his gaze off the mahogany wall to beam at his fellow tankers. Susan Glumm didn't mind being one of the gentlemen—she liked her job and it just didn't bother her. In her mid-forties, twice divorced, holding up well— resembled Diane Sailor, if you squinted—dated younger men…life was good. You'd expect her to say something like, "Go ahead, call me one of the boys! I couldn't give a rat's ass."

"But Bob, could it be better?" boomed Bateson.

"Could always be better, Gil," Bob coolly said. Bateson couldn't rattle him, they'd known each other for many years; had worked together most of this time. Though he was in his early fifties and he wasn't a husky man like Gil, Bob was solid, inside and out. As accountants go, Pridgeon was tough; he knew the feel of cold…hard…cash, life's blood.

"Yeah, could always be better, right, Reg?" Bateson asked his neat, nervous, and young General Manager of the Technology and Manufacturing Group. "Got any news for us, Reg, something to brighten our future?"

"I wish you'd address me with my proper name of Reginald. I don't know how many times I've asked you." This was something he could safely request—it was a close group.

"Sorry, Reg."

"Anyway," he sighed, "we're about to release two new Swiftee microprocessors for low cost PC's that run at 1,600 and 1,800 megahertz—or one point six and one point eight gigahertz, however you want it—as you know, as well as the three chipsets and the flash memory products mentioned in my memo dated August 23. What's that thing I always say, what was the…oh, yes, that would be, cutting edge. Any questions?" Reginald asked with a smirk, as he sat in the large, green leather cushioned chair with his elbows on the table, hands folded under his chin. He turned to face each member one by one, from left to right, and after he'd collected all of his blank stares, concluded with, "Well, if there are none, then thank you, lady and gentlemen." He was sensitive to name and gender issues. The others were sensitive to his sensitivity—edgy, uncomfortable, uneasy, along these lines—but still, you had to listen, he knew his stuff, and he was Gil's Nerdbot.

"Sounds great, Reg…inald. Well, Sue, are we gonna sell this stuff or what? How 'bout the old stuff, can we still push that?" Gil addressed the baggy eyes of the Sales and Marketing Director, who happened to be very hungover and rather slumped over the table with her nose propped up by a cup of coffee.

"Well, Gil honey, we're not coming out with a whole lot of new product at the moment. It appears to me as if we should do some re-packaging. I've done another SWOT analysis and it looks like we should name—or rename—our line of chips after Spanish Galleons or something else with a string of Hispanic names. A little market broadening should net us a few more of the wetback bucks," she sighed, and took a huge swig from her cup, not taking her eyes from it.

"You tellin' me that these Mexicans now have the cash to buy computers?" Gil inquired with a slight frown—to have to think about these things was not entertaining, but necessary.

"The American Hispanic population is growing rapidly and making more money, thanks to a strong economy. We need to get on top of this," she explained, massaging her eyes with her right hand. "This was all provided in that memo I sent a week ago."

"A week ago, oh yeah, now I remember." He couldn't recall, but what he knew and didn't know was his own damned business. His job here was to stoke the fire. "Well, let me know the names you come up with, okay, Susie?"

"As soon as they're ready, boss. Anyone got some aspirin or Tylenol?" she pleaded, ungluing her eyes from her coffee and meeting the eyes of her colleagues.

Reginald was quick to reply, before the "Naw, nope, and sorry," with, "Yes, Susan, I've got 100 milligram, micro-coated aspirin. Would that do?"

"That'd be fine."

"How many would you like?"

"How 'bout three?"

"Here you are," he said, handing her the tablets.

She popped them in her mouth with such quick flick force that they were propelled to gag central at the back of her throat, and this organ did protest. After much coughing—which did tend to help clear the head—she swallowed the rest of her cup and resumed original posture.

"You okay, Sue?" Gil asked, knowing the reason for her condition, having benefited from such an experience on countless occasions, as did everyone else—though Reginald wouldn't admit it.

"I'm fine," she replied, gazing up briefly to give Bateson a flash of a grin.

"So, then, that leaves us with Matt. Matt, my friend, what have you got for us?" Matthew preferred to be addressed as Matthew, but since he was new—had been with the firm only about a year—he felt that it wasn't yet his place to voice his preferences. He could be Matty or Mathilda for the outrageous salary he was drawing. And he stuttered.

"I'm ma, ma, ma, looking aah, aah, aah at a couple uh, uh, uh," he consistently began his presentations with an introductory bout of stuttering. Everyone was used to this and simply watched him—somewhat sympathetically—and bobbed their heads unconsciously with each stammered syllable, "at a couple of real sluh, sluh, sluh," they were often not sure what was coming next. Gil and Susan were thinking "slut"; Reginald was expecting "sloppy" for some unknown reason. "Sleeping beauties!"

"Outstanding! What have you got? I know you haven't e-memo'd any of this!" Gil insisted with intense eyes, imagining himself to be salivating.

"A company called, Real Chipper, would probably be a friendly takeover with an offer of seventeen dollars a share for fifty-one percent ownership," Matthew stated, as he was warming up. "And Prochip would be hostile, but I think we can swing it."

"Fuck 'em! Do we need these companies?" Bateson asked, almost breathlessly.

"We need them," replied Matthew. Despite the stutter, he was as cutthroat as the others—more so really—for his was the meanest, most vile job. Tirekicking, buying up companies, re-shaping them through right-sizing (downsizing), getting rid of the dry holes, and all kinds of other mean, nasty, ugly things.

"We got the juice?" Gil asked, knowing the answer. He was on top of cash flow and debt.

"We got the juice," said Matthew, negotiating yet another verbal curve with stammerless elegance. Bob nodded his head in thoughtful agreement.

"Gentlemen," Bateson concluded, "that about concludes today's business. It appears that there'll be a little less competition out there fairly soon and we'll be increasing our profit." He gazed around the table making eye contact with each earnest executive and asked the ceiling with raised voice, "WHAT'S THAT MAKE US?"

"BIG 'N HARD!" they shouted.

Chapter 3

Les hadn't been back to the Bay Area but a few times since he'd moved up north to Seattle. Duchamp Avenue in Berkeley was three lanes of one-way and there was usually available parking after six P.M. Same mix of high school and college teenagers, along with a few late-seeders in their early twenties and some real ancients, trying to relive the freely forgotten love of the 60's by bumming spare change—squatting on sidewalks before head shops, music stores, and pizza by the slice shacks. He wasn't certain if that was the same Bubble Lady of twelve years ago, but the bubbles were fairly familiar. Same stands along Telephone Avenue selling beads, silver jewelry, leather wallets, beaded jewelry, bongs, pieces of leather, Grateful Dead T-shirts, strings of beads, and other things cool. Had to be something a Bohemian could and would assemble or want to buy. High-tech, electronic gadgetry was kept in the closet—not for sale, don't tell anyone we use it, okay, man? There was a stride too…long steps, slow, shoulders dipping to the sides, head cocked back, mahnn.

So, Les Vincent had time to watch the locals or local impersonators practice being hip thirty years after it happened. And it was very relaxing, he had the time, he was early. Les'd planned to be there ahead of time, so he wouldn't miss anything. His hotel room was a mere two miles away, by the marina, so it wasn't as if he would have been late or something. Perhaps it was the fear of being rushed, or simple rush aversion. He wasn't sure, but it always seemed to happen. And mulling over this fact was killing the experience, yet again.

After strolling past many new sights and smoked memories of this side of the Berkeley University campus, he finally decided to go upstairs to Pip's Pizza, where he could grab a beer before the others arrived. Casual...no rush.

Seven-thirty on a Friday night and Pip's was beginning to fill up. Les was keeping pace as he worked on his second mug. Tracy arrived first—bouncing in, short blonde hair, hint of make-up on a very cute face, on a very cute neck, shoulders...all the way down cute. And fit. Fat fled from her in a frenzy. She instructed aerobics as a profession and she used oxygen real well! Also recently divorced and currently un-seeing. Les was aware that she, as well as he, was among the solitary unseen, but it was not to be that the twain should meet. Theirs was one of those extremely comfortable friendships in which there was no possibility that romantic interest would peer through the crack in either of their open doorways. No voltage there.

"Les," she said with high-beamed face, as she approached the table, arms spread, swooping swiftly, "it's great to see you."

"Great to see you, Tracy," getting the words out as he rose and was embraced, aerobically embraced. Hugged by a veteran hugger; very well squeezed. They sat.

"Do you still drink beer?" he asked.

"Every once in a while, I'll bend an elbow," she admitted.

"Let me go up and get you one. Any preference?"

"Cold," she replied, thinking that was a respectable response—a Berkeley-in-the-80's call.

"Be right back," Les said with a grin, thinking, "Good call."

They sat at their window table overlooking Duchamp, updating each other. Tracy discussed life as a recent divorcee—having lost her ex, a wealthy businessman, to his young, voluptuous secretary. It wasn't the fact of it so much as the vulgarity, she claimed. How trite could it be? Was she destined to live an already-been-done life? Alimony was useful, though.

Les talked about the wonders of Puget Sound, for the most part. They'd seen each other since he'd moved and his former existence was stowed silently away. The topics of trees, trails, boats, fish, and other pursuits of a nature boy made for decent, light beer conversation.

And then Steve showed up in a big way. As he always did. Not that he meant to—Les and Tracy had never met anyone as laid back as Steve. A six foot five, 280 pound black man had little option—unless he was showing up at a Really Big Dude convention, fashionably late or otherwise. Big way.

Steve Williams was a sight for their eyes. Even though he was Les's close neighbor up in the Seattle area, they got together only about once every couple of months. Steve's straining eyes almost popped their sockets with Tracy's grappling greeting—she was also glad to see him, you could tell. Les hadn't yet reached his threshold of beer for non-female hugging, so they shook hands. Emotion such as this can be draining, more beer was obtained to replenish.

He was toasted. To good friends by Les and to good times by Tracy. Rather common themes to celebrate, but these people weren't out to impress one another with cutting-edge, fast-break, cerebral material. This was not some performance, they were not on stage...just friends getting together. Not trying to do any one-up-man(or woman)ship. Nothing to prove here.

Tracy and Les had him de-briefed in all of about seven minutes. They could recite everything regarding his wife, kids, job, vacations, and recent purchase history, until finally he had to say, "Hey, keep your shirts on, I'm not going anywhere. Why don't we get another pitcher and relax for a while. I've got to save some material for Ben and Ashley, okay?"

"Yeah, okay, Steve," said Les, always willing to yield to the beer option. He was a tad embarrassed at his participation in the general grilling—but sometimes you get caught up. His eagerness for the scoop only revealed his current need to *get a life*. Though he had nothing to prove, he did not feel the need to reveal more of the fact that he was not living the ideal life. Nobody ever really did want to bare themselves in such a way, but he didn't want to let them think that his was so extraordinarily less ideal than theirs. Though it probably was.

"Sure, Steve, sorry," replied Tracy with a smile, and she polished off the last of her mug. It wasn't embarrassment that she felt. She had been determined to keep the topic of conversation off her, wouldn't wear well. "My turn to buy and fly," she said, as she got up to fetch a pitcher.

As the beer progressed, they regressed, and were living their lives in the student co-op once again. This was comfortable accommodation. Back at Burlington Hall, the dregs of the co-op system. This was where you usually wound up in the beginning; it was a huge former apartment building—1930's vintage, housing over 200 students. Many of them freshmen, recently released from their parents.

Affordable living in return for less luster and five hours of work a week. You were assigned a job or jobs that you knew, could be trained for, you liked, or any or none of the above. The students did everything: cooking, cleaning, administering, switchboarding, repairing, you name it—and frequently under the influence.

Burlington was a hell of a first step into adulthood—almost a sidestep or detour. No parents, and, wow, see all the kids here to play with. Fertile ground for retreading.

Ashley and Ben completed the quorum by around nine, late and lagging without the time difference. They'd come by air and shared a cab from the Oakland Airport. But it felt strange to them to spend this kind of money, even if it was split. The alternative transport was the BART—after a shuttle from the airport—to one of the Berkeley stations; it was a short cab-ride from there. And the locals called it just BART—dropping the "the." BART didn't waste money; saving money was what they'd done in the old days, in the co-ops. But they weren't poor students anymore—she was a corporate attorney, he was a corporate scientist—they could afford it, no sense living in the past. Still felt weird, though.

Pip's brought them perilously close to the precipice of history. This had been their main hangout during those collegiate years; drinking far too many spirits was what they frequently did back then and there. And you can only neglect your past, or former lives, for so long, Friday night, back in Berkeley.

The easiest way to consume beer is to remain stationary, this was well-established theory. Places that push this beverage upon their patrons tend to incorporate this concept in their design. Their insipid arrangement of bars, stools, chairs, and tables casts a mysterious hypnotic calm upon them—luring their guests to remain, weakening their knees, and…drinking beer is an excellent thing to do when you're sitting there, doing nothing.

"Okay, everyone," Ashley announced, clapping her hands a couple of times, "enough with the reminiscing. Let's relive some of it, let's play the game—the Bullshit Game!"

"Bullshit Game?" wondered Tracy.

"Oh yeah, Bullshit, I remember the Bullshit," remembered Les. "Full name being something like, 'The Bullshit-That-Really Pisses-You-Off Game.' Am I correct?"

"I believe you've nailed it, ol' Buddy," said Steve, with one of those pseudo-sincerity grimaces.

"What's the category?" asked Ben, ready to get on with it and hoping to avoid too much of that afterglow that people get when they discover that one of their mental faculties hasn't completely gone down the crapper.

"Each of us chooses one," said Ashley. "I'll go first. Let's go philosophical, something highbrow…television."

"Gaping intellectual hoop, that one," noted Steve, with his grimace.

"Okay," said Ben. "Me first. Let's see…way too many talk shows rerun late at night with too many mouthy, overweight, overly-inquisitive women interviewing very unfortunate, under-educated guests with incredibly strange problems and missing teeth."

"Fat too," added Tracy, shaking her head.

"Don't forget that guy, what's his name? Everyone ends up fighting—Ringer...Stinger?" said Ashley.

"Yeah, him, the guy who ends his show with his words of wisdom," Steve said. "Unbelievable. We're living in God's humorous nightmare!"

"I'll go now," said Les. "Newscasters who actually think they have a wonderful sense of humor and insist on sharing it over the air. This characterizes most of the herd, I believe." He glanced over at Ashley to see her response to what he hoped was his witty repartee.

"Yeah, they are still doing that," agreed Ben. "Been doing it forever; caught on even before college. Who goes for this crap? Is there some group—large group of idiots out there—calling the stations or responding to pollsters, 'Gosh, I simply love their humor, finest material I've ever heard. I sure do admire that intelligent television personality! And show me more commercials, will ya?'" Ben eyed Ashley to see how *he* was doing.

"Unless they're pretty—man or woman; the pretty ones are the straightmen, they smile or chuckle," Tracy remarked. "They don't have to work as hard."

"What about the guy—national news—who says his L's funny?" asked Ashley. "Should that be legal?"

"Legal and it makes sense," concluded Steve, "with everything that's happening in this world. There should even be one out there who stutters. That would also make a whole lot of sense." He was nodding his head thoughtfully, and the others chimed in silently with their nods and sincere faces.

"My turn," said Tracy, excited. "How about this? TV personalities—absent from programming for decades, out of the public view, people making jokes about them—who suddenly appear with their own shows, as if nothing had happened!" She was noticeably exasperated.

"Yes!" agreed Ben, audibly.

"Seems like the networks are real hard up!" said Steve, as he cracked his knuckles above his head.

Les turned to Ashley; he agreed, but he couldn't come up with anything to add—he opted for the thoughtful nod with head aslant.

"You go, Steve, okay?" Ashley requested. "I haven't got one yet."

"All right," he consented, "let's see, well, my kids watch cartoons, right?" He paused.

"Sure," "Right," "Of course," and "That's your excuse," were comments made.

"Anyway, yes, I see them too. But the quality? Nothing like Bullwinkle out there these days. But what really irks me…many of them are really toy commercials! Prolonged toy advertisements!" he said, with a wrinkled brow and no grimace.

"It's a crime!" insisted Les.

"A shitty deal," added Tracy. Despite this sad news, the evening was going well for her—no further mention of her divorce or life or anything.

"Ashley, you're up," said Ben, wide-eyed.

"Um, well, I guess it's the boobs," she declared, and made sincere eye contact with each player.

"Do you mean bosoms or buffoons? Plenty of both being broadcast," Steve inquired.

"Boobs, tits, cleavage!" she insisted.

"Big knockers sell," Tracy agreed.

"And this is a problem?" Les quipped, and kicked himself for it mentally.

"Might be for you if it were balls," Ashley returned. "You wouldn't like it if there were too much emphasis placed on the bulges, would you?"

"Yeah, no, you're right," Les said, hoping to recoup, reminding himself that his purpose was *not* to make an asshole of himself.

"Pandering to the lowest level," concluded Ben, content with the way this comment went.

"Okay, folks, next category. What do you say to politics and politicians?" asked Steve, and all agreed.

Fertile ground there and they waded through this category without much difficulty, holding their noses, and having increasingly greater difficulty comprehending one another. Not because they were holding their noses, but the hour was getting wee and the night was pounding their nerves dull. They made tomorrow's plans and made their ways home.

*

The group had been lucky with the tide, early the following afternoon. It was out far, at Fitzgerald Marine Reserve, on the coast south of San Francisco. You needed a low-cut tide to see everything. Timing was also an important factor if you wanted to catch a view of things intertidal. An early morning low tide meant little to those who'd arisen late, with tenacious hangovers. This mistress of the sea that frequented the sand bars south of The City was feeling flirtatious this day. They'd cradled their cups of Pete's coffee, goofed up on extra strength aspirin or equivalent, as Tracy had driven them from Berkeley, across the Bay Bridge, over to Pacifica, and down the coast a few miles. One of those miles—the mile of falling rocks and tight turns—made for some beautiful viewing, if you had the stomach for it. They didn't. There was a nude beach along this stretch too. Again, their stomachs and maybe a few other organs wouldn't permit.

Purple Shore Crab, Aggregated Sea Anemone, Bullwhip Kelp, Turban Snails—all of the main characters of the intertidal scene—were shown in a glass-covered display by the ranger station, next to the parking lot. Les knew this material fairly well because of his backgrounds in biology and zoology, so he gave it a brief glimpse. The others took a little more time, perhaps to assure themselves that they were in almost no danger of being swallowed whole by a voracious, intertidal, man-eating sea slug or something.

A wayward tide at Fitzgerald exposed a reef covered with algae, water-filled depressions, and many brightly colored beasts, most without vertebrae. There were a few fish—some sculpins and an eel— who had the backbone, tolerance, size, and camouflage to hang out at the beach when all their friends had made the offshore commute. But these were fish living on the edge.

As designated intertidal driver, Les brought them out onto the reef and demonstrated the key survival technique first thing—avoiding the slip. With the exception of what is called Nail Brush, the algae on these rocks are really damn slippery. Les showed them the Reef Step, known to assist those having difficulty negotiating with seaweed. One of the slickest of the bunch, Sea Lettuce, is also edible. Les ate some as the rest watched because he assumed that the ability to consume unfamiliar objects was a talent much to be admired. The others assumed he was way too hungry.

They split up to forage for the sights of the shoreline in two contingents: Ashley/Steve/Tracy were drawn west to the tideline by the dark silhouettes of the Sea Palms and splash; Ben and Les began flipping rocks in search of crabs.

"That's a Porcelain Crab," Les informed an excited Ben, who had majored in genetics—many forms of life were strange to him. But show him some bacteria and he was right at home. The crab, his first beach trophy, was safely returned.

"And that is a Brittle Star," Les told him of his second treasure. This type of starfish had long, thin, active arms. "You're getting lucky!"

"Yeah, it's been a while for that," Ben admitted.

Being fairly certain that Ben was not referring to his luck in unearthing or unseaing invertebrates, Les said, "You and me both, Dr. Kramer, you and me both."

"Isn't Ashley looking good? Not that Tracy's…Tracy's an attractive woman, but I've never…well, I'm not attracted to Tracy. And I never was to Ashley, but now…now she is lookin' pretty fine," confessed Ben, as he poked at a Giant Green Sea Anemone.

"Same with me," admitted Les, with a shrug and furrowed brow.

"Why now? Desperation?" wondered Ben.

"Different circumstances. Back then, we were surrounded by women, most of them single. Too much potential back then—a trees-versus-the-forest deal," saged Les.

"I guess you're right, we couldn't see Ashley for all the trees," replied Ben, moving to another spot along the pool's edge.

"Too much to see, too many options. And now here we are," stated Les, arms wide, gazing up to the sky.

"Yeah, a couple of heavy hitters, but I think you're right about the tree thing. Ashley's looking pretty pleasant without all the other trees."

"I may be right," laughed Les, shaking his head with an enormous self-effacing grin, "but who the hell can tell?"

"Still, Ashley is more attractive. I wonder," Ben paused to ponder.

"Is she seeing anyone? You should know since you live down there, near her." Les asked with little doubt what Ben was pondering. He had been considering the same thing himself.

"Nope. All clear," stated Ben, as he tasted some Sea Lettuce.

"Well, there you go," Les replied, trying to disguise his own interest.

"Sspphitt, sspphitt!" Ben responded, ejecting the algae in what people do when they spit. "This stuff does not taste good, does it? I mean, it's not just me, is it?" asked Ben in protest.

"An acquired taste. It's better with beer."

"Anything's better with beer, you schmuck!"

The others were kneeling next to a Sea Palm, admiring it while getting sprayed by the waves.

"What?" shouted Tracy. It was difficult to hear over the sea noise.

"I said, okay they're little palm trees, let's get back some; I'm getting soaked!" shouted Ashley. The three began their return, doing the Reef Step with arms outstretched, shoulder-height. This version was the Gliding Gull Reef Step—a west coast thing.

They went back in the direction of Les and Ben, who were tidepooling fifty yards (or meters) out from the beach, concentrating on their feet, bypassing much of the intertidal life.

"It really bothers me the way TV news reporters end their little piece from the field with what they think is a witty closing, using opposites," Tracy commented, her mind suddenly having backed up to the previous evening's Bullshit. "You know, something like, 'Things would have been all right if these crooks hadn't been so wrong.' You know?"

"Things might have been different if they weren't so much the same," Steve said with a smirk.

"Well, not quite that inane," replied Tracy.

"I know what you mean, Tracy," said Ashley. "I can't think of one right now. Probably better to try to forget about it anyway." She had algae on her brain.

They completed the rest of their high-wire waltz back to the other two, where Ben had made yet another discovery.

"What's that little yellow glob?" he asked, pointing.

"Hey, all right, you sir have found a rare creature. That is a nudibranch," announced Les, slapping his friend on the back.

"A what?" inquired Steve.

"A nudibranch," Les replied.

"I gotta see this," said Ashley. "I don't get out much." She stepped her way between the two kneeling by a pool. They all admired the golden broadcast from the few centimeters of slug with a bouquet of gills extending from its back.

As is typical for many a day along this coast, the sky was clouded and the wind whipping. This band of tide steppers soon became tired and hungry—nothing to go with the Sea Lettuce—so it was time for the beach picnic portion of the outing. Deli sandwiches and iced tea—watch for gulls bearing gifts.

Conversation ceased, and there it was, like those recordings you can buy for relaxation, no sound but the waves and the odd gull. This gave them opportunity to hear their own thoughts, instead of that insistent nagging voice, urging them to keep up with the current yack because the yak and the cart were getting way too far ahead of them.

"Why isn't more of life like this?" wondered Tracy.

"It is if you choose it to be," Steve responded, pouring sand onto sand. Les took a deep pull with his lungs and blew out the air. Ben followed suit, digging deeper with his pull. Ashley looked at him, hoping he wasn't sitting on some enormous, undisplayed sand creature, or something else unsettling.

"And it's free," Ashley proclaimed, raising her arms in an air embrace.

"Something even I can afford on a middle school teacher's salary. But I specialize in the low cost outing. No chasing after the Jones to the fancy resort—let 'em run, I say," quipped Les, making a theatrical gesture with his right arm and index finger.

"This is a fairly popular belief these days," Ben agreed, "but I think there's some merit to it. People should stop hunting down the almighty buck."

"Leave the damned herd alone," Steve added.

"No, I mean it," Ben continued, bordering on irritated. "Do we really need the fancy cars, swimming pools—all the goods?"

"I like nice clothes," admitted Tracy, feeling in a confessional mood.

"But you could do without, couldn't you, if you had to? Could you trade in the fancy duds for more free time? With the kids, if you had kids?" Ben asked.

"Well, no kids," said Tracy. "It would be an adjustment, but I suppose I could get used to having more quality time, even if it wasn't well-dressed quality time," she conceded.

"Be better for the planet," Les added. "Everyone's heard this—less consumption, less production, less pollution—it might be a lot greener around here if we'd slow down."

"You're right, Les," Ashley said, nodding her head, kneeling on the sand.

"It's like we're all caged hamsters on those wheels. We keep 'em spinning and spinning, and all we get for it is more junk cluttering up the cage," said Steve.

"Hamster wheelin'," agreed Les, accompanied by a group sigh.

Quiet toppled over the group as before. It was as if all were making a concerted effort not to do anything that might be considered as being consumptive, so that all of those desirable things that were said might be realized—to get off the wheel, free of the cage. Or maybe they were just too pooped.

"Buy less and live more," stated Tracy, still stuck on the Bullshit.

*

Fully rested from their hotel rooms and freshly removed from BART, walking along Market Street in San Francisco, it was Saturday night in North Beach.

North Beach bustles on a Friday or Saturday night, and the scheme had been to find a place with a worthy, live band and no cover. They could afford to pay an entrance fee, but where was the challenge in that? And you had to be able to move—the bar couldn't be too popular. You couldn't judge a dive by its cover—not the charge, but the facade—most of the spots in North Beach had that scuffed, needs a paint job, weathered chic appearance on the outside, and often in, too. Perhaps the proprietors were thinking, "if it ain't broke...," since they seemed to pack 'em in and they weren't going broke themselves. Anywhere in The City was the draw, they could slide on that. Lou's seemed to fit the bill and the price of drinks wasn't going to bust their illusion of being thrifty.

Dark and loud with R and B, capacity crowd at the bar, but a few tables free. Some folks were out on the floor shuffling near the band, so the stage fright ice had been shattered. Ben and Les alternated dance duty with Ashley, with the occasional request for Tracy, who didn't feel that she needed the exercise. Steve held court at their table. He preferred the kick back to the heel kicking and also made a reasonable deterrence to those who would abscond with their precious real estate. Conversation was not an option in that din, but loud comments and nodding made for passable table communication.

They left Lou's after about an hour because of the heat. Actually because of the sweat—who likes sweat when your clothes aren't for gym—but it is more delicate to complain of being overheated. You can't complain of too much sweat, since there is never too little that you're going to admit to—you leave it alone.

Steve remembered some neighborhood-type bars on Columbus Avenue, so they headed that way to cap off the evening with conversation that consisted of more than squawks and head bobs.

There was one such place across from Washington Park. No ferns, no fancy artwork, no frills—a no-nonsense bar except for an old jukebox and a small hanging TV. No customers either.

Ben bought the first round from a bartender he imagined to be named Joe. Late middle-aged, white T-shirted, and chewing a cigar stub, Joe could be found in no other bar and no other bar like this could be without its Joe. A fact that assured Ben there was at least one thing he could count on—he'd taken on a bit too much of the Blues from the previous place. Those Blues had clamped onto the others, as well. They sat around a small, round, red table.

"It doesn't seem to end. I'm in debt up to my carefully shaved armpits," complained Tracy.

"Who isn't in debt?" Ashley replied. "It's a fact of being these days."

"I'm not in debt," confessed Les, "but I also don't own a house. Guess I mortgaged my future with too much school and little chance for it to pay off."

"What have you got to complain about?" asked Steve. "Each one of you is single, without children. In addition to the mortgage, I've got to feed, clothe, and entertain a family, though my wife helps a lot, that's true."

"But the point is," Ben said, "we really could live without debt. We don't need to have mortgages, new cars, wall-sized TV sets, state-of-the-art sound systems. We just do."

"Popular culture," Tracy commented.

"Why do you think it's so popular, Tracy?" Les asked.

"People simply like high-tech stuff? I don't know. Maybe because there's so much merchandise out there…"

"Because we can," asserted Ashley. "We can buy all the fancy new things because we can borrow the money, very easily."

"Why do we?" asked Steve. "Why do we buy all these things?"

"Everyone else is," said Ashley.

"Getting dizzy here," Les said, thinking how clever he was being. "This discussion is so circular—getting dizzy here."

"We get you, Les," Tracy declared. "You sure it's not the Tequila?"

"It's greed!" Ashley stated, so astounded at her revelation that she glanced around the table taking in each friend's facial response.

"Greed?" said Steve. "How do you figure greed?"

"It makes sense," Les said, glad to be of Ashley's assistance. "We know that some people are more greedy than others. The greed, what is it—an emotion, a feeling—well, being greedy could have been an advantage, evolutionarily speaking. Those more greedy in the past were able to obtain and conserve more resources for survival and reproduction."

"So now we're so greedy our greed is eating up the planet?" asked Tracy.

"Guess it's one reason for many of our troubles?" Les replied, sincerely.

"Does it get worse, do we keep on being greedy, buying what we can get away with? This may be overly dramatic, but—living empty lives?" Steve asked.

"There actually may be something we can do," said Ben.

Chapter 4

Pike Place Market was one of those bargain hunters' tourist attractions set in old shipyard warehouse space, so it had the popular antique look and people went there because the idea had momentum. Fairly fresh seafood and produce could be hunted there at low risk of high price. Gil Bateson often insisted that one of the Core Group members accompany him there for lunch.

"We may need to make another offering to get enough cash for the Prochip takeover," Bob Pridgeon said, as they walked past the long row of arts and crafts tables at The Place.

"Shareholders'll bitch about that," Gil replied. "How about taking on some short term debt and doing a little preemptory—say layoff some more and hire more temps. Could also change some benefits—say screw the dental, give them some bullshit reason for it." They stopped to watch some fish mongers chuck salmon at each other as they made boisterous commentary—one of the benefits of being a bonafide fish market—somewhat similar to feeding time at the seal tank, the exception being that the flying fish were caught with the flippers here, not the mouth.

"I'll look into it some more. Another thing might be to do all of the above," offered Bob, as he passed by the neat stacks of iced Dungeness Crabs.

"Let me know what you come up with by Thursday. I'm kinda in the mood for some space—I lust for layoffs," Gil proclaimed, patting Bob on the back.

"Speaking of lust, Bob, how's the Pre-nup holding up?"

"Well, she's thirty-five, looks thirty-five—can't complain. She's good at parties, doesn't embarrass me. I do my bed duty, but she's not too demanding. She's a retread, you'll recall."

"If there's one thing I do vis-a-vis personnel, it's to keep up with my Core Group's relationships. You're not only my friends—only friends really—but relationships can affect business."

"Of course."

"Anyway, yes, I know your Pre-nup, what's her name? Oh, yeah, Patty. You signed with Patty three years ago, March. She'd had the big D about nine months previous to that. Am I correct?"

"Amazing. Yes, exactly right. How's your adornment?"

"She's a bitch, nothing's changed. Like yours, she performs her functions. Don't know if she knows about what I've got on the side. Doesn't matter. I give her a couple of years."

"Time for a trade-in?"

"You know the drill," Gil answered. They went downstairs for lunch with a few microbrews, each feeling better for having had the opportunity to make a personal connection with a fellow human being.

*

If the sky was fairly clear, Bateson would change the venue for the scheduled Core Group Meeting. Instead of the boardroom, they'd meet at his sixty foot Ketch, moored at Shilshole Marina, or somewhere downtown Seattle. Another month, another meeting plus rain equaled the boardroom.

"Gentlemen, as you can see it's raining again," Gil announced cheerfully, "so here we are. Here is where we happen to be, but WHAT ARE WE?"

"BIG 'N HARD!"

Bateson persistently attempted to bring variety to this opening dialogue, forever trying to introduce the rallying question in novel ways. Though they always anticipated it, the Core Group never failed to be surprised and delighted at Gil's innovative panache.

"Let's start with Reg."

Reginald had to open with a big sigh, yet again.

"Our concentration right now is on a new line of even faster chips. We're talking about speeds in excess of 1,900 megahertz. This is a highly competitive area—processor speed, Susan tells me—so we're trying to hold the edge over those other bastards!"

"Well said, Reg, way to go!"

"Thank you. So, that's about it really, concentrating in this area," Reginald stated with a confident stare into his boss's eyes.

"So, Reg, what you're telling me is that we are concentrating on these faster chips at the moment," Bateson surmised, wisely.

"Yes."

"Then I guess that about sums it up. Let's see, how about the world of sales and marketing; what does that world have to say, Sue?"

"The Niña, Pinta, and Santa Maria have set sail! All we have to say is *Ole!*" she said, slowly twirling her right index finger by her ear. Susan's eyes were less than clear and seemed to sag from too much baggage. "And we're going to make these chip ships even more popular with a catchy commercial. Picture this: photo of the Niña, then a photo of the Niña X chip, then film of a soccer goal with that Spanish announcer shouting that familiar *GOAL*; then photo of the Pinta, same series; then the same for Santa Maria, with a long trailing *GOAL* shout at the end. Came up with this at a Mex place last night. What do you think?" she asked, eyeballs straining.

"GOAL!" Gil shouted, arms thrust skyward in football fashion. "Gentlemen, your comments," he requested with startling return to composure.

"Fine," "Ga, good," "Should do." Heads motioning agreeably.

"All right, moving along," prompted Bateson. "Matt, you're up."

Worst possible timing, Matthew could feel the choke below his vibrating tongue revving up for one helluva percussing performance.

"Ra, ra, ra," he paused, knowing it was futile at this point, but was also aware that Bateson expected him to do something verbal. His option was not simply to sit there with an oddly contorted face. "Ra, ra, ra." Another pause. We've got two cheerleaders now, Bob was thinking. Yeah, I agree, thought Susan, but Reginald's mind refused to comment.

"Real, real, real." Whole entire words, this was a promising sign. "Real Chipper and Prochip have been purchased, as you are aware," he suddenly spurted with amazement and sudden confidence. "They are currently being restructured in the usual fashion, downsizing being accomplished through substantial layoffs, rehiring some of these same workers as temps to save on benefits, etc. Again, we can get away with this for a couple of months until things settle out and we know better how to proceed." A silent group sigh ensued.

"Excellent, Matt, excellent! Okay, yes, good news, lightening the load! Bob, you're up," Gil said, clenching his hands together in a prayer-like pose.

"Thank you, Gil. Gentlemen, there's not much to say that you don't already know. We've done a little downsizing here at BNH, you know that. Initially we made a secondary offering of two million shares. Well, as of today, we've upped that to five million—this with the Board's latest vote. Should more than cover the recent acquisitions and leave us with a large cash reserve in case this sleeping giant wants to bed another sleeping beauty," he said, with a company-eating grin on his chops.

"Yeah!" cheered Gil. "Fuck the competition! Is that it, Bob?"

"That's it, Gil!"

"Well, HOT DAMN! HOT FUCKIN' DAMN! This makes me glad—makes you glad—but what does THAT MAKE US?"

"BIG 'N HARD!"

Chapter 5

He couldn't shake it. Day after day, night after night—those dreams were never dreamy. In any case, that weekend trip to the Bay Area two weeks ago had left him befuddled with all-consuming passion for Ashley. Silken red hair, shoulder length—that body, that soul, mostly the body—it was too much!

What he needed was the hook, the reason, something reasonable, some way to convince her to see him soon. He had no time to fashion this hook at work because at work he was consumed with genes. His mind at home seemed always to have the *Occupied* sign showing and if he'd had the guts to open that door, he would have seen the very woman of his pining. Couldn't concentrate, out of focus.

During one of those rare and endangered moments of lucidity, he came up with a plan, an ingenious scheme, the stuff of rocket science—an idea that just might work, possibly. What had been the final topic of conversation that night in Joe's bar? Greed. Consensus was that something should be done about it. And what was it that he was currently doing the very science on? Well, it was aggression, how to block aggression. But what was one of the main side effects of the treatment? Less greed! Treated mice were not only much less aggressive, they were also much less greedy—they shared their food. Then he had another revelation. He then recalled that he'd thought of this, without mentioning it, that same evening. He slapped himself mentally, for a change. The hook though, now he had THE HOOK!

The place was on Goleta Beach, north of Santa Barbara. She'd had another meeting up there, so everything had fallen into place nicely. Dinner on the water. The first three answers to the question of how to attract the future Mrs. or Mr.—location, location, location. Ben often confused real estate with courtship.

"All right, we've got the shrimp, the bread, the wine. I'm fine, you're fine. This is the moment," Ashley said, "now I must know. How do we do it?"

Ben liked the way she'd put that. His mind wandered under the sheets, by the surf, in the bushes—his thoughts got a room.

"Ben?"

"Yes, well, do it. Yes, the greed gene. We can block a gene that has an influence on greedy behavior, I'm fairly certain," he said, zipping up the image of his fly projected from his cerebral circuit board.

"Fairly certain?" she wondered, drinking some wine in hopes of improving her comprehension. "You're only fairly certain?"

"It works on mice. It likely works on humans. Couldn't really hurt to try, I should imagine."

"You should imagine. When did you start *should* imagining anything? Where'd this *should* come from?"

"I don't know. I guess it sounds more cultured to say *should* something, instead of only something. *Should* imagine, instead of plain imagine," he said, and shrugged.

"Make mine plain, okay?" she requested, and had some more drink—comprehension vastly improved. "So, how does it work?"

"You mean how is the gene blocked?"

"Yeah."

"It's fairly complicated. If you think we can get the others involved—they sounded interested anyway—it might be easier to describe the procedure only once," he said, gazing at her hopefully. He wasn't in the mood to give a genetics lesson.

"Don't think I can handle it, huh?" she asked, eyes downcast; somehow she seemed slightly dejected.

"No, no. Briefly then, I've isolated a mutant protein that attaches to a brain cell and prevents it from signaling aggressive or greedy behavior."

"Now, was that so hard? I get it," she exclaimed, showing a hint of exasperation.

"If you're happy, I'm happy," he replied, happy to have avoided the details.

"But," she said.

Oh God, he thought.

"But how do you get this protein into a person?"

"That's a good question."

"Thank you."

"You can inject them with it; that'd be difficult to pull off. You could spray them with it; they may not like that."

"What about in their food?

"I don't think so. No, not as far as I know."

"Okay, we can discuss this with the others."

"Do you really think they'll be up to doing something as devious as this, something probably illegal?" Ben wondered, himself feeling a foot chill coming on.

"Let me rally the troops, get them back to San Francisco. I'll get them primed, you can convince them," she nodded with confidence.

"You really want to do something like this?"

"I am a success, Ben, but I am unhappy. I am unfulfilled. I live in L.A., Ben, the world is the shits!"

"I see what you mean. Yeah, the world is in the dumper," he agreed, wishing she'd lean on him to make things right without having to commit a highly illegal, possibly immoral—definitely dangerous—act of social engineering, or whatever it was called.

*

Despite all of its gaudiness, the vulgarity of Fisherman's Wharf was not to be missed. But it was fun! The Armada Inn was decided upon because as a hotel chain, it had predictable accommodations. Though they were possibly about to embark on a thrilling adventure—one fraught with many unknowns—they still hadn't shed themselves of their need for some control over their environment. You don't have to expect the unexpected—hence the Armada.

The hotel sat by the sidewalk at the southern fringe of The Wharf proper; that is to say, you had to go at least a block north to find a store dedicated to those highly sought-after Wharf goodies. It wasn't far—so it still counted—they were officially at The Wharf.

It was magical, really, that feeling that came over you at The Wharf. Your mind went for a quick dip in the bay, leaving you defenseless against the onslaught of tourist traps that had you cornered at…The…Wharf. Which used to be called Fisherman's Wharf, but Fisherman—and his partners, if there had been any—sold away the rights to the name about five years ago. And the new owner, who wished to remain anonymous, had an eye for a bargain, an ear for a trend, and the cash to back it up; the new owner renamed it to, "The." Many popular TV game shows at the time—one at least—were dropping their first names, succumbing to the popularity of, "The." Everyone in the group felt the need to go touristing before getting down to business, so they found themselves eagerly stalking the shops and stands at The Wharf.

"Ever since we played that game of Bullshit, TV is pissing me off more and more," Tracy admitted. In a fairly tight formation, they had formed a five-person, mobile obstruction, certain to dismay those pedestrians prone to sidewalk rage.

"Don't watch it," Les said, the others laughed.

"Yeah, Les, we've got so many hobbies. I don't know about the rest, but I find myself less and less able to commit the amount of time that I feel I should to watching The Tube," Ashley responded. Les wanted to borrow that tongue pressing against her cheek.

"I know why overweight women are so popular for talk show hosts—or older women, for that matter," Ben offered.

"Answers to important questions of the day," Steve replied. "Don't make us wait any longer. I'll just die of anticipation," he said, placing the back of his left hand to his forehead and shutting his eyes.

"Women are big TV watchers, make up a huge portion of the viewing audience," Ben began.

"Damn, it was so obvious! Thanks, Ben!" Ashley interjected. The others understood her words, despite the fact that her tongue was occupied elsewhere—in the land of the cheek.

"Let me continue," Ben said, eyeing her to assure himself that she didn't mean to be cruel. "Big portion, women are…and…fat lady hosts, or old ones, don't make them jealous. They can watch those hosts because they aren't sitting there being jealous of those hosts. Make sense?" he asked, gazing at the rest of the sidewalk squad.

"What about attractive ones then," Les inquired, not entirely convinced.

"They're stupid."

"Ben, you mean to say that women viewers aren't jealous of attractive female TV personalities because they are stupid?" asked Ashley, as she watched her shoes avoid all the lines in the concrete.

"Women TV viewers are stupid?" asked Tracy to Ashley's question.

"Well, yes, but I was referring to stupid women on TV," corrected Ashley.

"That is my working theory," Ben stated. "We see much of what we see on TV because it doesn't make women jealous. And I am not being sexist."

"Works for me," Les commented. "I don't think you're being sexist."

"Neither do I," agreed Ashley. "Ridiculous maybe, but you are certainly not sexist, Ben Kramer."

"Well, that's okay then," Ben replied, doing a little tongue-in-cheek dance of this own.

One thing though, at The Wharf, there was a surprisingly decent offering of fresh seafood. Each squad member purchased and consumed an over-filled shrimp sandwich, much of which was intent upon taking up residence on the side of the cheek that the tongue never met. Sloppy, yes, yet a necessary component of a proper Wharf tour package. Next on the itinerary was a sound clomping around on an old sailing ship, followed by a stop at Ghirardelli Square; a quick in and out at the Maritime Museum—along with the ship, the cultural parts of the tour—Ripley's Believe It Or Not, and far too many overcrowded shops, densely packed with cheap imports or At-The-Wharf-Collectibles that you were justifiably compelled to purchase.

The bay breeze compelled them to Golden Gate Park and Steinhart Aquarium—seldom visited by them as BU students—but a must for Tracy and Les, who had grown up in the Bay Area. So two fifths of the assemblage needed a trip to the aquarium, an urge almost like spawning salmon to the home stream.

Through the main door and straight to the gator pit. Les informed the others that he and Tracy might have actually seen some of the crocodiles and alligators before.

"You mean it, sincerely, Les?" Ashley implored, loudly jarring other animal onlookers, having grasped him on the upper arms and probed deeply into his eyes—needing to know. Abrupt sarcasm never failed to take Les unawares, and as it was doing this, the other aspect of the gesture—the not entirely subtle flirtatious aspect—passed him right by, out the door, and across the concourse to the Japanese Tea Garden.

"Yeah, they can live fairly long," he replied, braving a return stare.

"That's real interesting, Les," said Ashley, with a puzzling smile. Les was puzzled; the others weren't playing, they'd moved onto the loop around The Pit to view the caged snakes, turtles, toads, and salamanders. Ashley let go of his arms, finally.

Les had difficulty getting over that mystery smile and the upper arm grasp duration. The latter seemed to have extended beyond some sort of bounds. He puzzled over the meaning and description of those bounds, and the smile. Perhaps, he thought, she only wanted to shut him up.

"It's really great to see you again, Les," Ashley declared.

"Yeah, it's great to see you too," he replied. He hadn't had much practice with this sort of bewilderment lately, but he couldn't panic. He didn't panic and as luck would have it, or so he presumed, he knew a fair bit about reptiles and amphibians. They walked the loop discussing these fascinating creatures, having a fairly fascinating time, at least one of them knowing what, if anything, was happening. After completing the round, they followed the others past the huge, dead Great White Shark on display, and proceeded into the darkened halls of illuminated fish tanks.

After the fishing trip, they decided to follow that flirtatious aspect of Ashley's gesture—the one that crossed the concourse—so they ended up at the serenity of Japanese perking and pruning. The music concourse was an area dug into the ground like a sunken living room with really quite bad furniture. Park benches—built before the term *ergonomic* was invented—were lined up in rows, shaded by close-cropped Fruitless Mulberry trees, facing a Roman or Greek bandstand built in 1900 called the Temple of Music. The promise of caffeine was too much for Steve and the women, so they didn't step on the grass directly to the tea house. Ben and Les headed left, perhaps because the Japanese Tea Garden is located north of the equator. The Coriolis Effect dictates that water must drain clockwise north of the equator—they were composed primarily of water—so this was the circular path onto which they were drawn. Or, it was the steeply arched bridge to the left that was begging, in Japanese, to be climbed. Either way, the two found themselves free of the others.

"They do use too many breasts to sell things on TV though, you've got to admit that," Les told Ben.

"I do? I guess so—sure, cleavage is all over the tube," he admitted.

"Bet that's not the case in Europe, though, they're not as fixated on tits. Why are we fixated on tits?" wondered Les.

"I don't know, but I sure like 'em. Not implants though, won't go for the fake ones," said Ben, as they passed some Bansai trees.

"Me too. But I heard in the news that an implant saved a swimsuit model's life, by taking a bullet."

"A brave breast implant? Now there's an idea—boobs with personality!" The garden's beauty was so serene.

"Why stop there? Make implants with utility—include radios or lights in them," said Les, thinking that they really shouldn't be taking this hike back into adolescence.

"How about alarms?" Ben suggested, wondering what force was carrying him so far from adulthood.

"Sure, or computers?"

"Can you imagine what kind of keyboard?" Ben continued, never ceasing to amaze himself sometimes.

"Well," said Les, "back to sanity, grown-up talk." Ben was glad someone had said that and so was Les. "But you've got to admit, Ashley's got a nice set," he added, sly grin and all.

"Ashley is a woman of lovely proportions and a generous soul," replied Ben, knowing he now had the upper hand on the maturity road that both were eager to get back up on—at least before they found the tea house. Each now felt certain that the other had a well-proportioned, amorous interest in the fetching Ashley Bradford.

*

Pier 39 seemed to have recently appeared to Tracy. She figured that the new Pier 39 could have been no more than fifteen years old, which placed it in the recent category, since those years hadn't made much of an impression.

The Pier had been selected for the dinner venue because of the high probability that they'd find a decent restaurant on the water where they could dine with no reservations. How bad could it be? This was The City and that was The Pier. Seated with drinks all round by seven.

Ashley had done much of the mouth-work by telephone, which was why the former co-op club had reconvened so soon. Not that she wasn't an effective attorney, but not much convincing had been necessary. Tracy was always up for something. Les had felt stirrings and special feelings upon his last encounter with the redhead. Life at home for Steve needed a breather. He wouldn't say much about it, but he had experienced recent marital lack of bliss and too much pressure from some overtightened screws in his section at BNH.

Even so, Ashley felt the need to repump the audience before Ben elaborated. She got them grieving over greed, poverty, spiritual emptiness, anything that sounded somewhat on topic—television (why not?), overconsumption, pollution—fifty percent divorce rate, growing gap between rich and poor, gun control, video games, etc., etc.

"There's a reasonable chance that at least some greed, some greedy tendency, in humans can be stopped biochemically for say, two to three months per application," Ben said quietly, staring down at his water glass.

"Ashley said something about that, Ben, what are you talking about here?" asked Steve, uncharacteristically. Usually he sat back and watched the others stumble through their conversations. This topic was doing something for him. Ben had the attentions of the others corralled, as well.

"I've been working with a gene that produces a neurotransmitter, a molecule that signals a nerve cell. This neurotransmitter—we're calling it atsamine—is only released during times when a mouse's resources are in short supply. It signals nerve cells to stimulate or initiate certain behaviors like aggression, or as it turns out, greed, as well," Ben stated and shrugged.

"So," Les said, "the gene codes for a neurotransmitter, atsamine, that stimulates greed in animals?"

"In mice, very probably humans, yes, that sums it up," agreed Ben.

"How can you stop this greed gene from doing its business?" asked Tracy.

"We don't touch the gene itself, but we can make its product, atsamine, ineffective," replied Ben, over the persistent barks of the California Sea Lions. It's not that they disputed his claim about the greed gene, or what was on the menu for that matter. No, this was merely some haggling over parking spaces on the dock below—a bit of dock rage. Window seats at The Pier could have a downside.

"Okay, so how do we take the juice out of atsamine?" asked Ashley, who was dying for the end of the story.

"I'll try to make this as concise as possible. There is a strain of mice at Tailored that are highly aggressive and greedy. It turns out, through my work," Ben said, working up something of a fervor—perhaps the mere thought of the pressure at work, "that the gene responsible, the greed gene, is found in different forms. The normal form of the greed gene produces a type of atsamine that binds to a nerve cell receptor, stimulates the nerve cell, and then degrades after a short time, so the cell shuts down. We have preliminary evidence that the same interaction occurs in humans. Mice in this aggressive strain have a different form of the greed gene that produces a neurotransmitter that binds to the receptor, but doesn't degrade for a long, long time—these mice are effectively always greedy." The sea lions seemed to have negotiated their space allocation treaty on the dock, so Ben decreased his volume—a matter of security. "By subjecting individuals of this strain to mutagens, we have produced mice that are never aggressive—their form of the neurotransmitter is a molecule that binds for a helluva long time, like the non-mutated, aggressive strain's and it is non-toxic, but, but it does not initiate signaling in the nerve cell. That means it does not stimulate aggressive or greedy behavior. And since it is sitting there, bound to the receptor, a normal form of atsamine, if it were present, would not be able to do a thing. The greed gene would be blocked," he concluded, raising his eyebrows unconsciously. It was effective, however, ...that look. The combination: that look with what he had set before them said something like, "Jesus, this is some powerful shit we've got here!" There was a pause.

"And this will work on people?" asked Steve, with a sitting- on-the-edge-of-his-seat face.

"Probably," confessed Ben, with a definite tone to his apprehension. "Oh, yes, I forgot to add, I have cloned this mutant form of the gene."

"Okay," Ashley prodded, "so...you said that it could be injected or sprayed. We can't go around poking needles into people, that would not be legal. I can't see myself walking up to someone and spraying them in the face—that's just not done. I also can't see us delivering the spray into a building's air conditioning system. So, Ben, how do we apply this stuff?" The others appeared less convinced that this was, in fact, the next step.

"Question before that, I think is, should we apply this chemical to someone," cautioned Ben. Sea lions had no comment.

"Humor me, Ben, if we think we can do it, then maybe that will help us decide if we should do it," she implored, in a mild way. Normally, Ben and Les would have been keenly aware of all the "do it" mentioned, but they were too immersed in genetic ethics.

"All right, I have put this to some thought. The answer is perfume or cologne. I clone the gene into an adenovirus expression vector. We place a solution of this into cologne or perfume bottles. If all goes well, we have got a product that, when it enters the circulatory system via the nasal mucosa, will stop the greed gene for two to three months.

"So what do we do, mail it to someone and hope that they use it somewhere close to their face?" asked Tracy, ever the practical espionager.

"Wait, I know," insisted Ashley, "a sampling stand. Set up a stand—same idea as when you walk through a cosmetics section of a department store and some employee sprays you with a tester. Do the same, except with a stand outside some building, like a promotional."

"Sounds as if that should work," said Les in support of Ashley, hoping to gain some turf over the acreage that Ben had amassed with all of his biochemistry.

"Well, should we do it?" rallied Ashley, under her breath over the table.

"Hold on, Ashley," cautioned Steve. "Who would we do this to?"

"Someone real greedy, so we can see the effect," Ashley replied.

"Can't be too famous," said Tracy. "We couldn't get close to a celebrity."

"Whom do we know who exhibits extreme avarice?" inquired Les. Ashley might admire a more powerful vocabulary—worth a stab, he thought.

"Oh, avarice," commented Ashley.

"A person who demonstrates extreme greed, a person whose everyday decisions impact many people; someone who is not a celebrity," Steve said, as he was winding up.

"Someone who stinks of greed," said Tracy.

"Someone who needs us to take away some of that stink," said Ashley, coaxing the table's approval with her fist.

"I know that person!" blasted Steve.

Chapter 6

Susan Glumm had wanted to slow down and pick through the vegetable stands at Pike Place. Mostly from guilt grown by a lifestyle of feigned hard work and a determined, prolonged happy hour. She wasn't a member of AA—not being much of a joiner—but she was beginning to wonder how many nights of bar clinging and boy toying she had left on her calendar. Plastic surgery could shave off only so much of that persistent morning malaise—she was really starting to show her whiskey.

Lunch with the boss was always interesting, better than remaining in Renton as one of her restaurant's regulars, anyway. Bateson was forever in a hurry to get there, and once a *there* became a here, another there to get to. Gastrointestinal distress was a footnote to the job description for one of the Core Group at BNH. No time to linger by the spinach with a fleeting notion of a healthy diet. A handful of vitamin supplement breakfast and four sublethal cups of coffee never managed to sustain Susan to the midday meal, but always had to do—another of the ruts she stumbled along. Her body parts quaked and grumbled past the nagging vegetables as she high-stepped, keeping pace with Gil.

They swerved and entered what was formerly an apartment building that had been partially gutted and converted into an antiqued mini-mall, complete with worn carpeting and stairways of questionable integrity. Another darkly-paneled bistro with a menu that would not fail to provide a lunch, like the lunch obtainable at neighboring minimalls in dark-paneled places with menus.

"Black, Hispanic, white, Asian, I don't discriminate," stated Susan, in response to another of Bateson's nosy, keeping-abreast-of-things-that-should-be-kept-personal, interrogatives.

"How many different ones do you have…say…in a week?" asked Gil. This was fascinating dish; she was a handsome woman. Susan'd never nail him for sexual harassment or anything—these were innocent questions, and they were old friends. But sometimes these conversations with Ms. Glumm were highly educational, like letters printed in *Hustler* or *Penthouse*—highly educational. Bateson had a vigorous and satisfying social life of his own, but hearing about some of Sue's saved him on valuable reading time.

"One at most, but hey, listen, what do you think this is? I had a boyfriend last year, remember? I'm not a damned hooker!" she demanded.

"Yeah, you're right, sorry; I get kinda carried away. You live one helluva life, Sue!"

"Well, thanks, I guess," she replied, unthankfully.

Their waitress, a small woman in her early twenties, with chin-length, straight, thin, brown hair on a skinny skull and frame, approached their table and placed the menus before them.

"Good afternoon," she said. "My name is Stephanie. Today's specials are…"

"We don't need to know that," interrupted Gil. "We'll order in a few minutes, bring me a scotch and soda. Sue?"

"Glass of white wine," she ordered.

Stephanie scurried off.

"Shop talk?" Bateson asked, and sipped some water.

"Fine."

"You memo'd something about public relations," he said.

"Yes, Gil, I think your, our, public image could use a boost. Maybe it's time for you to donate a large sum of money to some worthy cause."

"I guess it's about time, isn't it," replied Gil, staring into her eyes and nodding his head slowly. His closed mouth was turned down in earnest commitment to social welfare. "It is November, the write-off season is at hand," he said with a whimsical glance up to the motionless ceiling fan.

Stephanie arrived with their drinks and placed them before each.

"Today's specials..."

"Hey, Stephanie," Bateson blasted, "your name is Stephanie, isn't it?"

"Yes, sir," she cowered.

"Stephanie, I asked you to give us a few minutes. Was that a few minutes?"

"No, I guess not, sir," she replied, eyes almost shut.

"Don't guess, Stephanie, that is not your job. Your job is to serve. To serve well, if you want to keep your job. Now go away and come back in...a...few...minutes, okay?" he asked with an annoyed frown.

"Yes, sir," she said, and sprinted clear.

"Stupid little bitch," he concluded, and regained the composure that he hadn't really lost—barking being one of those necessary means.

Lunch survived the motions. Most of their discussion revolved around the sales and marketing of computer hardware, which is why Gil had hired Susan Glumm those many years ago. She put the dip on the computer chip with a few choice words and images—she could get those dips to buy anything. Part of the reason she could still make points on the saloon circuit? She'd perfected persuasion, personal or otherwise—and the booze didn't hurt.

"So where's the check? That little skank's not doing her job again," complained Gil, so as to be overheard. They were still here, and there was waiting.

"She's over at another table," said Susan, pointing.

"Miss," called Bateson. "What was her name?" he asked Susan.

"Stephanie, I think."

"Stephanie," he hollered.

"I'll be with you in a minute please, sir," was Stephanie's hushed reply, after she'd placed some plates on the table and stepped back, so as not to disturb these customers.

"Incompetent little bitch," remarked Gil to Susan.

"She's not that bad," replied Susan, unconvincingly. Susan could really care less.

"This isn't a bad little place, with the exception of the hired help. Might be interesting to own a little restaurant here at Pike Place. What do you think?" he asked.

"Yeah, maybe."

"I think I may look into buying this little establishment."

"You've got the juice."

"Yes, I do have the juice," he admitted, with that wise nod. "Then I'll fire that little bitch!"

Susan could really care less.

*

Gil's ketch was really a refreshing place to have lunch when it wasn't raining, gull factor included. The CEO would often have lunch with Matthew Zonk at the marina because there were fewer distractions. The Director of Corporate Business Development found that it was easier for him to *spit it out* in the absence of disapproving eyes. Though it was less convenient—he had to get take-out and the driving time was almost double—Bateson found that he could make a helluva lot more money when Matt was able to complete a few sentences. Anchors aweigh.

"I, I, I," Matthew said, and paused. Gil was thinking again about the way Ricky Richardo would respond to one of Lucy's guffaws.

"I, I, I," Matt tried again, and stopped. This time it was the lyrics to some Spanish song that were running through Bateson's mind—as they usually did during the second round.

"I think we should get into video conferencing. It's hot and we won't have to retool. I'm watching at a couple of companies that seem ripe for the picking," he finally blurted. A moment of silence.

"Video conferencing?" replied Gil. "Hot, is it? Yeah, I guess so; all those fools out there that actually want to see each other when they're talking. So, you think you can make us some money?"

"I think so. The two companies a, a, a…"

"That's okay, Matt, you can memo me the details," Bateson interrupted, suspecting that this was one of those days. Important matters aside, it was time for Matt's reward—a period of quiet consumption. The established routine had been for them to swab through the shop chatter, as soon as they stepped on deck, then it was time for the rations. As they sat across from each other in the cockpit, if it were a windless afternoon, it took all of their effort to muffle their mastications—attempting to eat in total, unembarrassing silence. They ate real slow.

"So, a couple ready for takeover in video conferencing, eh Matt?" Gil remarked, wiping his mouth with a paper napkin.

"Yep," he replied after a swallow. "Yep" was a fairly safe bet, one short syllable.

"What a day, eh Matt?" said Bateson, stretching his arms. "Great sky, great scenery…quiet. Can't beat it, can ya?"

"Nope."

"Real invigorating. Makes you wanna go out and eat up a couple a puny companies, don't it?"

"Yep! Yep!"

"Yeah," Gil smiled, contentedly.

*

Cubicle sprawl, a field of square space. Very tall people found them amusing and easily negotiated labyrinths; they could see over, gave them some small sense of confidence. The 1980's solution to high rent and the need for personal space—pack 'em in, but make it seem as if they're in command of their own territory—old warehouses made trendy.

Why those partitions weren't made higher, no one knew. They did create visual isolation for most office space men and women, but the very tall employees got to peek. The average Joe/Jane cubicler was aware of this fact; it made them kind of nervous. Even though a firm might not have any attitudinally-advantaged persons on the payroll, the rest knew that that day would come—climate control set to apprehensive. Steve Williams wasn't a doorway ducker, but he could make a reasonable head-count at close range when he stood in his cubicle at BNH.

"Good morning, Steve," said a short, wide, bald-headed man, as he met the partitioned space. Fred Gompers made the rounds usually in the morning—not because he felt that he would have better command of his employees still recovering from the previous night's torpor—but because he was a morning person. The rare morning person had morning legs that needed to be taken out for a walk, so they didn't get all cramped and grumpy. Grumpy legs tended to shuffle and fidget under the desk, or so current Morning Person theory claimed—bad for business.

"Morning, Fred. What's up?" said Steve, as he swiveled in his chair to see the General Manager of the Microprocessor Products Group, his boss. Steve was one of twenty-five computer engineers who worked in MPG. The running joke was that the firm got good mileage out of the MPG. They hadn't been hired for their sense of humor. Which might have been a problem, since it probably took a substantial one to face those gray, sound-sucking partitions eight hours a day, five days a...hell, why belabor the labor.

"Just got the word from above, got a few minutes?" Fred asked, rubbing his scalp with both hands.

"Sure, Fred, have a seat," Steve replied, saving the material on his desktop. Fred sat.

"These are sure strange times in the computer industry," Fred began.

"You don't have to tell me," said Steve, knowing that good news wasn't described at the get go as being strange—hot or fantastic, that would mean good news. Strange meant that something bad was going to happen, going to happen on a need-to-know basis. This wasn't mere gossip that Fred was passing on, this was a news item not welcome in Steve's personal space. He hoped that another very tall person wasn't taking any of this in.

"As you know, Steve, BNH has made a couple of recent acquisitions, The, uh, Prochip and what's the other one?"

"Yes, those two chip firms. Yes, I know," said Steve. He knew that Fred was going to ease into the news; they'd known each other for about seven years or so. Steve was one of the more senior engineers in MPG, and Fred was a few years his senior there. The names of the two takeovers were two pieces of information that Steve did not need to know.

"Anyway, they've initiated another round of belt-tightening and we're being hit again—this time with layoffs," Fred said, with genuine concern in his expression.

"And I'm getting laid off," surmised Steve, clenching his teeth.

"Maybe, only maybe, decisions haven't been made yet. I thought I'd warn you that you might get laid off, even with your seniority and all."

"What basis are they going to use in their decision?" asked Steve, as if he expected some reasonable answer.

"Random."

"Random?" Steve asked, with a *what the hell* tone in his voice—and on his face.

"Random," confirmed Fred. "They use a random number generator in Human Resources to select employees for laying off."

"Sounds fair," said Steve, sarcastically.

"There is an upside. Many of those laid off will be eligible for rehire as temporary employees. Pay will be lower and no benefits, but at least they won't have to relocate."

"What would my chances for that be?"

"Oh, you'd get that opportunity, Steve; I'd make sure of that," assured Fred, with a warm smile.

"That's reassuring," replied Steve. "Thanks for letting me know."

Chapter 7

Ben decided that it was about time for him to take a more hands on approach to his life. Actions speak…he stopped there for fear of tripping over too many tired phrases. "Time to do something!" sounded sufficient—wasn't particularly clever—but it made the point.

He had to do it, it was imperative—as if some gene deep within his nuclei was turned on: do the deed, get the woman, reproduce, continue the species—but probably less dramatic, perhaps with no direct gene involvement whatsoever. Could have been a hint from one or two passing genes, such as "Damn I'm horny!" or something along these lines. Anyway, despite the danger, he'd decided to swipe a vial of the blocking atsamine—he'd decided to tackle the greed gene. Only because it would lead him into the arms of Ashley and whatever else became available.

The drive to work that Monday was like any other Monday's morning commute with one exception—this time he was packing cellular. He almost never brought the portable phone with him to work because he had no use for it. The thing had been purchased for emergencies, not simply to distract him when he should be attending to driving. But it was unloaded; he'd taken the battery out so that the space was there.

The secret to proper espionage was to remain calm—conduct the daily grind as it was daily ground—nothing unusual. He greeted everyone in his usual fashion, walking his usual way, stopping at the usual stops, thinking the usual thoughts, mostly, and driving himself to the edge with all of this *usual* crap! He was not spy stuff. Sweating at room temperature was a certain sign of this.

When it was time—he had not actually calculated the moment in advance, it simply appeared—Ben walked over to the refrigerator and withdrew a rack of vials containing the correct samples of atsamine. He grasped one vial, brought it up to the light—fluorescent light—overhead, and peered through it. Then he shook the vial and peered through it again. There was at least one security camera in his lab that he was aware of—might have been others; this examination of the sample routine was for the camera. A matter of security.

Ben brought the vial over to a lab bench where there were flasks, beakers, tubes, syringes, and other useful items, next to a sink. Specifically, he needed the tap marked DW for distilled water—it was green, couldn't miss it. He played Chinese Checkers with some of the flasks, beakers, and vials, as if he were setting up something important, and he palmed an empty vial. He then placed both hands—the one with the empty, the other with the vial of goods—into the sink, and acted as if he were manipulating something. When in reality he was—he poured one half of the contents of the atsamine vial into the empty vial and replaced this volume of solution with distilled water. Ben secretly placed the soon-to-be-stolen vial of goods into his lab coat pocket. The original vial, now diluted, was then used in another flask and beaker shuffle on the lab bench, returned to the rack, and the rack returned to the refrigerator. He went over to his desk and made some notes.

Like any other day, his day continued for another hour or so, until it was a reasonable time to go to the restroom. He didn't need to, but he needed to...he knew what he meant. In he went, vial and cell phone in lab coat pocket. He removed the coat once inside a stall, went through the typical procedure for having a sit, and sat. Having done so, he had the opportunity to check for bugs—was that the word—well, secret cameras. Not that it would have been possible for the folks at Tailored to even think of filming employees doing their private business—why was it called *doing their business*, anyway—but these days, better to check. Didn't see any, but he decided to complete the show, just in case. At the finale, he put on the lab coat and pretended to have trouble buttoning it—for this he bent over. In the bending position, he removed the contents of the pocket and inserted the pseudo-battery into the cell phone. Step two complete.

Ben couldn't take a vial from the rack and carry it home. Everything was recorded and there were checks. He'd never seen it done, but security had the option of searching anyone on Tailored Genetics' property. It wasn't going to happen, but it could. They weren't going to check the concentration of the now dilute original vial of atsamine, because there was no way of being certain what the concentration had really been. They were dealing with biology—things happen. Experimental error, a die-off, "this one must have had the scrapings"—many things could have happened. Nobody would check anyway. If someone were going to look, he or she would only eyeball the volume, at most! Ben couldn't focus now, his nerves were vibrating like cheap magic fingers on a motel bed—scary spy stuff. It was not an opportune time to try micropipetting, so he decided to get caught up with his notes; he was always staring at their backside, never managed to have them up to date. Ben sat down at his desk.

"Afternoon, Ben," blurted Eugene, who seemed to know of no other way to make his entrance, always an abruptly blurted greeting. No other way to blurt, but abruptly; the question was, why rattle the tubes all the time?

"Good afternoon, Gene," replied Ben, mentally placing a damper on his gonging nerves. "What's up?"

"Just making the rounds here," said Eugene, as he walked over to the lab bench for a brief survey. "How's everything going?"

"Fine, Gene, fine. I'm catching up with my notes. You know how it goes, let them get too far ahead of you and you don't know where you are," Ben answered, hoping that Eugene was having an awfully busy day, so he'd get the hell out of his lab.

"You've cloned that new atsamine, am I correct?"

"Yes, into the adenovirus," reported Ben, rising from his chair, walking to the sink, and washing his hands.

"Where is it? In the fridge?" asked Eugene, as he went to the refrigerator and opened the door.

"Top shelf," Ben replied, as he experienced some of those nagging second thoughts: why now, why me, why did I do this? An image of Ashley flashed before his thoughts, and he made a mental note, "Oh, yeah!" Eugene was peering through one of the vials, having already shaken it.

"Okay, Ben, so's this ready for more testing fairly soon?" he asked, as he replaced the vial and shut the door.

"Couple more checks and it's off to the animal facility," he replied with quaky confidence.

"Very good, then, very good. Okay, Ben, have a nice rest of the day," declared Eugene, as he swept out of the lab.

"Thanks," Ben volleyed, as his boss disappeared around the corner.

Past the gates at the end of the day and he'd done it. No more Mr. Nice Guy, he was now a corporate raider, of a sort. A spy. A man of intrigue. But it had to be kept on the QT, hush hush, say no more, or whichever current espionage lingo was fashionable. Others didn't have to know, he would exude an air of distinction that none would fail to miss.

This air didn't carry over on the phone line when he announced his success to Ashley that evening. Her reply to the news had been something on the order of "Good" or "Okay, then," and she'd marched onto the next stage of the plan. The plan that only she seemed to know. Ben was glad to hear her voice; glad for that limited amount of attention that was being deposited his way. His thoughts gasped every time she spoke his name—all three times. Ashley told him that she'd take it from there, make all the calls, and get back to him. He'd hoped for a meeting with her to strategize or something, but this occurred to him too late. Goodbye, click. Damn!

Chapter 8

That seductively scented fat wafting over the Food Court was highly persuasive to her purposely underfed frame. Tracy had to watch what she ate, even though she put in three to four hours of aerobics daily. Blind consumption of energy-packed morsels was careericide—this she kept repeating and repeating.

Christmas season at The Mall. This Mall was east of the Bay Area—perhaps even Bay Area proper, which was expanding, putting on weight—anyway, in the city of Pleasant Hill, where she lived. Like a cage full of ravenous mice, The Mall was a dazzling contrast to her 1,2,3,4 life. She wasn't a shopophile—claustrophobia having choked off any resource-gathering imperative directed by her genes to enhance survival and reproduction. Don't get me wrong, she told herself, I like the stuff—it's the process. This had been a slight source of angst for Tracy, especially when she was growing up, that she couldn't share the delight that her fellow sisters took in shopping—a missing link. But not shopping was not going to kill her. The reds and greens were attractive though. Who could fail to be impressed by the enormous Santa display erected in the Mall's middle? She didn't get out to The Mall much.

Her role on this day was as an observer. Tracy was on recon. About a thousand miles south of where the caper would take place, she couldn't shed herself of the notion that tight security must be maintained, that she must act as if she were actually out shopping. She wore practical shoes.

As an observer, she could not initially see the trees for the forest; had to get the overall picture first, get a sense of the layout—the trees were later. Five or six of your big name department stores, positioned at the extremities of the megastructure—avoiding competition and providing architectural balance. Small shops lined the wide walkways connecting the big boys, with foreign sounding or catchy names, specializing in: clothes, puzzles, just shoes, paintings, perfume, sunglasses, eyeglasses, toiletries, hats, nick nacks, candles, vitamins, watches, greeting cards, underwear, less underwear, small statues, or many of life's other necessities.

There could be no vacant real estate under the expensively domed ceiling, so expansive potted plants and artistic structures were shoved onto the walkway tiles, providing visual variety and some small degree of obstruction to forward motion—impeding the wayward motion of Mallers. And all those stands helped too.

A mid-80's technical innovation, shopping structure researchers had discovered that there was much marketing potential to be found in places where the customer is of an A-to- B mindset. Caught not entirely in a conscious state, it was found that potential purchasers easily stumbled into small impediments stuck before their stride—they wound up buying whatever found itself in front of them—hence the stands. A stand could feature: chocolates, calendars, animal paraphernalia, puppets, Hickory Farms (unless it was a shop there), art, picture frames, toys, dolls and small toys, just balls, fancy treats made on an actual farm, real estate, fancy gardening supplies, picture frames/key chains/pocket knives, or almost anything absolutely vital to your daily needs.

This component of her assignment complete—the big picture or forest—it was now time to focus on her target, get it between the crosshairs; it was time to get to know men's cologne. Anyone tailing her would have seen Tracy admire the layout of The Mall and shop at many windows without buying. Any real shopper would stop for a break at this point, so Tracy thought it best to stop for a coffee; there are not many calories in coffee.

Somehow the words "small" and "medium" had been retired from the vocabulary of beverages offered at bean houses, Tracy had missed the boat or bean-train on this one. This added an unknown to the equation—another setback. Coffee was now sized as large, grand, and something with one of those foreign names, but this was the biggest, venti. Tracy surmised that the shopping scientists must have found a significant increase in purchasing by really hopped up patrons, but she ordered only a large.

That extra burst of motivation coursing through her veins, Tracy nonchalantly proceeded to the nearest department store, a Macy's, and instinctively went searching for cosmetics on the ground floor. This concept really caught her eye, or some organ—how did she know that cosmetics would be on the main floor? She searched her memory banks for a glimpse of a cosmetics section that was not on a main floor of a department store and came up with a blank, a blank bank. She hadn't done much blankin' shopping for scent, but she knew—she knew that the main floor would be it! What a revelation! She made a mental note, the only type she could make in case she was being followed, "Cosmetics found on main floor, check there first!"

She found it quickly; she felt this was important because a seasoned shopper should find the product of her desire efficiently. Four oval counters, two featuring the products of single companies, the other two filled with the smells of many firms—one for each sex. These ovals reminded her of the stands that she'd had to negotiate around before arriving at Macy's, but these were much brighter. All those foot-candles had her almost blind, she was not dealing any mere…they'd taken out one of her senses, so she was forced to rely much more upon the nose—and now they were plying her with perfume. She approached the multi-firm men's oval and began mental notetaking: nothing special about cologne bottles except that they don't seem girly, no favored color to the glass, various volumes—say five ounces, a safe bet—and yes, there are testers. Filed it. She then picked up one sample bottle, smelled the spray nozzle, feigned utter disgust, and moved on to the next department store.

She concluded her recon after the third department store, a Nordstrom, perhaps a bit disappointed, yet satisfied. There had been little to distinguish the cosmetics sections she'd examined—they all looked so darn similar—this made her a little sad. It meant that, with the exception of a different scent producer thrown in here, a slight difference in price there, one cosmetics department was almost a clone of the next. Where was the variety, spice of life, the "viva la difference"? The world for Tracy became a little smaller this day, until she remembered that she didn't like malls much anyway—besides, what was with the coffee size thing? She had the required data. Mission complete. Time to get back home and out of the damned uniform.

*

Early December meant that school was almost on Christmas or Holiday break, so Les had to call in sick in order to conduct his assignment: to learn the daily/weekly routine of their mark, victim, dupe, the fall guy—the test subject, Gil Bateson.

Yes, the name of the President and CEO of Big 'N Hard had been suggested by one of its own employees and a member of this rag-tag band of crazy, impetuous social engineering wannabes—who had not yet thought of giving themselves a proper name, mostly because they wished to remain anonymous—none other than that highly respected computer engineer, Steve Williams. These were thoughts running, kicking, splashing, and otherwise having a fun time through Les's mind—before he put up a mental block to it—as he drove south on I-5 from Lynnwood, at six A.M. on a Tuesday morning, to Renton, where he would begin surveillance.

Background information provided by Steve, thermos of coffee (about two and a half larges or a little more than a venti), a small cooler with a couple of sandwiches, a small box of doughnuts (for quick energy and it was too funny to pass up), binoculars, a highly foldable hunting-type cap, scarf, sunglasses, waterproof notepad, and three sharpened, number two pencils. He was all geared up and he'd taken his vitamins that morning. Traffic was light and there was the threat of rain, but there always was, wasn't there.

Parking streetside, close to the converted warehouse that was BNH, proved to be of no difficulty. Les got out and cased the building, walking around the entire square block it occupied, in order to determine the locations of entrances, exits, and employee parking. He was told to watch for a bright red BMW, the car the CEO himself drove to work. Les wondered why such a wealthy man would stoop to drive himself, why no limo? And why a mere BMW? Steve claimed that this was the President's way of relating to his workers, suffering the common commute with all of its perils: the gridlock, road rage, and maybe a bad driver or two. This plan had actually back-fired since the BNH employees were not at all concerned about the boss having to commute, but they really liked the rich bastard's set of wheels; half of them took it as a sort of *in your face* deal. That bright red blinded them every time they went out for lunch.

After assuring himself that he would be able to witness all of the comings and goings of the mark, Les closed the car door, lowered his window a couple of inches, and poured himself a hot cup of coffee—about half a large. He'd developed the unhealthy habit of drinking a couple of quarts of coffee per day because this habit replaced his former habit of smoking. Every time he had a cup, it seemed as if something was missing from the uncupped hand. Les tended to down his java in no time, probably because his other hand was getting bored. On this day he had to ration the fluid carefully. This cup was gone in a few minutes. And before he knew it, he was asleep—at which point, it didn't matter if he were aware he were asleep or not. Another byproduct of a less harmful lifestyle—smoking's shaking and grinding having also taken a siesta.

All but a few of BNH's employees had been able to miss the snoring spectacle that was Les until about a quarter 'til noon. All but a few had parked three blocks east in the BNH parking lot, so they didn't see the slanted head, open mouth, and probable drool on the seat cover.

He awoke, checked his watch, and nodded to himself knowingly. Part of the job. This had been a warning, a shot across his bow, at least he hadn't attracted an audience. He would be fortunate, however, because for the most part, nothing would happen for the rest of the work day, except that a number of BNH employees would leave the building at lunch—Bateson not among them. There appeared to be a couple of cafes or restaurants at the other end of the parking lot, might be potential hot spots, noted Les, mentally. So the day had not been an entire waste, for now he knew two things: he didn't need to begin until lunchtime and there were a couple of eateries nearby that Bateson might patronize. And a third thing: he decided not to stay until the end of the day anymore—most folks only went home and it would be difficult to set up the cologne stand in Bateson's driveway. Had to hope he went out for lunch, and to some place less desolate than a couple of burger joints serving a parking lot.

The next day would prove even more exciting. The President and CEO, himself, would depart BNH around noon, accompanied by a smartly-dressed gentleman. They would speed off in the bright red BMW with Les in hot pursuit; this would be his first official tail. He would lose them, or rather they him, on Interstate 5 at one of the central city off-ramps. Another valuable lesson—why was it called a tail? Because it's stuck to the behind of an animal—it is on it, not merely some clump of fur wafting two miles back. Les reminded himself that Gil was probably not a professional tail watcher; he could stick on him unobserved.

The stake-out proved to be surprisingly monotonous. Bateson had holed up in the building the following day, but Friday ended up testing Les's tailing skills—car and foot, this time. Gil and a solid, medium height, high-end middle-aged gentleman parked in the lot at the north end of Pike Place Market, next to Victor Steinbreuk Park. Les maintained about a ten foot space behind them as they walked slowly past the long, canopied row of stalls along Western Avenue. As he mirrored their actions—stepping slowly, stopping at times to admire the merchandise, Les picked up some of their conversation. He managed to hear them through the scarf, sunglasses, and oddly perched hunting cap; he had forgotten his trenchcoat.

"They're part of the package, Bob, your adornment ain't adornment without a big set," said Gil.

"I know, I got Patty done two years ago. They look great, I can't tell the difference."

"Well, Bob, even if you could tell the difference, even if they were more squishy, or what have you, they are a necessary item. You can't go to a party with flat-chested adornment, Bob, you can't. In order to maintain your status, or maybe even improve it some, you need to have those hooters; big tits mean power!" Bateson asserted; Les caught a glimpse of his wrinkled brow.

"Yes, I know, Gil, even with all that shit about a health risk," said Bob with an amused snuffle.

"Hell, everything'll kill you these days. They won't pick up any cancer for at least five years after the job, so it doesn't matter anyway; they're already on the recycle heap."

"And, they may not even get it. Could be that nothing happens to them," said Bob, on a positive note. "Then everyone's a happy camper!" Les shuddered at that gleeful phrase. He was averse to popular phrasing, even more put off by this than the other things he'd heard up to this point, strangely.

"Everyone's a happy camper...hello...it doesn't matter...that's why God invented insurance," insisted Bateson.

Les felt a considerable degree of nauseous after that last use of a greeting word for emphasis.

"Hey, how 'bout this puppy!" Bateson said, holding and tilting a very narrow, blue liquid-filled, plastic thing. It made bubbles. Mention of the popular young dog word was all he could take.

"Jesus!" Les exclaimed, staring up at the canopy. Both tailed men turned.

"You got a problem, pal," said Gil with a sour tone. Les grabbed the first piece of art in front of him; this happened to be a carved female hoola-dancer that would shake-it on the dashboard.

"Jesus," he reiterated, "I gotta get one of these!" And with a proud face, he turned to present his treasure to the inquirer. Both businessmen turned away and continued their saunter.

Les hurriedly looked at the piece, looked at the expectant young woman on the other side of the stand, and said, "Damn, I forgot, recently got one of these from my aunt Thelma. Nice one though, nice one." At which point, he replaced the wooden object and rushed, nonchalantly, to catch up to those ten feet behind his tails, or tailees.

They entered the connecting walled mall, passing art galleries, import boutiques, boutiques for baths, antiques, flowers, cafes, hat huts. As Les was following, he couldn't help but notice all this merchandise was typical for the middle of any mall. He saw them enter Pike's Bar and Grill and then he left. The Market was a possibility.

Monday was another bust—Les could have spent his time doing something better than car sit while he avoided smoking. Bateson emerged with a Blonde—who resembled Diane Sailor in a holding-up-well, middle-aged, high maintenance sort of way—on Tuesday at noon. Since he was experienced with the tail, Les had no trouble following them to Pioneer Square to watch them enter some sports bar and grill with a name like T.J. McRowdy's, or something similar. The Square was off the list—no decent, plausible spot where a cologne stand might be found. Seemed like a pleasant place for a drink, though.

Wednesday and Friday were lunched at The Market, so that decided the matter. Thursday had been very interesting, however. Not from the caper's standpoint, but from a personal interest, gossip, *the dirt*, aspect.

Thursday started out like any other stake-out day…but with a twist. His mark, Mr. CEO, had more on his mind than a meal at noontime on Thursday. He left BNH alone. They drove—in separate cars—up north to Alki. Les parked on the street about a block from Bateson, watched him go to the door of a condo with a view of Elliott Bay, and knock. The dark, poofy hair of a woman, with a fair load of eye-makeup, appeared halfway up the open door; the two embraced, closing the door as they back-stepped, as a coupled unit, back inside. It must have been at least seven minutes, but no more than ten, when the front door opened again and the two emerged—she with even poofier hair—and walked a couple of blocks farther down the road to a cafe. Les knew that Bateson's home was in Eastside, so this was not his wife. He doubted that she was a sister or a cousin, from that embrace. Might have been excessive Christmas affection, but he doubted that this had been a seasonal display. Then he shook, rattling out of the soap opera that was happening in his head…purpose…this was not a place for a perfume stand—move on. He bet that they were, in fact, doing it, though. He knew about these things, Les was almost a professional.

Chapter 9

"Solipsism," Ashley repeated to Tracy, as they sat around a table in the bar at the Homesteader's Inn, Pioneer Square, Seattle.

"Nothing exists but what I imagine?" Tracy asked. Steve's eyes widened, as he silently engaged in their conversation. Ben and Les had their own going.

"That's the theory. Nothing exists or is real, but the self," replied Ashley.

"Then I must be really messed up!" Tracy confessed.

"It's only a theory, Tracy, doesn't mean it's a fact," Steve offered.

"Well, what if it's true?" she pleaded.

"Then you are really messed up, Tracy," Steve concluded, shaking his head slightly, as Ashley nodded hers.

"All the fat ladies on TV, the idiot shows, now the moronic money game shows…growing gap between rich and poor, gun control, video games, etc., etc.?"

"All your fault," said Steve.

"Then I need some damned help!"

"I think we all do, Tracy," said Ashley. "I've got an idea," she said tapping Les on the shoulder to get the entire group's attention, "Let's go for a walk around the square, find another bar, and finalize our plans for tomorrow?"

"Sounds good to me," Les replied, and all concurred as they rose and made for the exit.

It was told that the original "Skid Road" was, in fact, this Yesler Way that bordered The Square. Only a couple of drinks, so they weren't ready for the "Road"—too busy watching their steps on the bricks of The Square. Walls of bricks surrounding them, western style streetlamps and an old trolley stop—artistically bent iron. This was The Square. Bars, billiards, Italian, coffee—and lots of art, many galleries for the artistically bent. This being the Holiday season, a plethora of twinkling lights poked through the fog.

"She's looking damn fine," said Ben.

They were a few steps behind Steve and the women. Les replied, "And we haven't even had too much to drink. I, myself, find her heat to be hot."

"But still, not Tracy."

"No, not Tracy."

"I don't know why, not Tracy."

"Because she's like a buddy that you really get along with. Doesn't have that mysterious edge."

"I know what you mean. No mystery there. But she's damned fine."

"Just no mystery."

"No mystery."

"Too chummy, you know? If she were to be naked all of a sudden, your first thing, you'd turn your head away," Les predicted.

"Well, not right away," Ben stated.

"Not right away, but soon."

"Soon."

They ended up in T.J. McDundee's, a sports bar, filled with successful Sunday shoppers, Sunday drinkers, and lonely Christmastimers. Walls of wood and mirrors.

"So, Les, you've got the white tablecloth and the card table, right?" Ashley inquired, from the other side of the booth.

"Check," Les replied.

"Be serious," she admonished. "Leave those with Ben."

"Tracy, you're all set with the cosmetic salesperson clothing? Red, am I right?"

"Yes, red, Ashley, Like I said over the phone," Tracy answered, slightly annoyed.

"You're going to hold onto the spray bottles, right Ben? Two identical bottles with water and one larger bottle with the stuff."

"Yes, that's correct, Ashley," Ben said, sounding earnest.

"Thank you, Ben, at least you're taking this seriously," Ashley said, and gently patted him on the shoulder. His eyelids dropped in gratitude. Steve thought, what about him, for a second, but he wasn't that desperate for attention. He'd supplied the women with some photos of Bateson; his role at this stage was minor, had to keep out of the picture—he could be fingered.

"And we all have cell phones, speed dials set, correct?" Ashley addressed the assemblage. Nods and "yeps" followed.

"Okay, I guess we're all set; anyone got anything to add?" she asked, powerfully.

"Yeah, who made you the boss?" Tracy wondered.

"Well, since I've been…" she stuttered, and Les interjected.

"Ashley has been the glue for this whole thing, Tracy. She's the one who made all the phone calls, all the arrangements. I think she is kind of the boss."

"Yeah, it's okay, Tracy, we need someone in charge," Ben added, looking up at Ashley.

"I vote for Ashley," said Steve, shaking his head in wonder at this high schoolishness.

"Okay, me too," said Tracy, relieved of her concern.

"Let's have a toast," Les said, holding up an empty glass, "but first I need another drink."

"Maybe not tonight, Les, okay?" Ashley said. "We need to be fairly alert tomorrow, and you've got a fair drive home tonight."

"I'm crashing at Ben's," Les replied. Ben glanced at him with a questioning face. "If that's all right with you, Ben. I can sleep in a chair."

"Yeah, fine with me, I guess," Ben responded, hopes of a night with Ashley going down the skids.

"So, then, we'd better call it a night. All agreed?" Ashley said. Nods and "yeps" followed.

They walked back across The Square to the Homesteader and Steve left them to go home. The remaining four lingered in the lobby for a few seconds—the men hoping for more action, the women being polite. Those seconds passed, enough time for Ms. Polite Manners from the newspaper to have given the nod, so Tracy and Ashley grabbed the next ascending elevator. Les and Ben were left staring at each other, wondering about the next move.

"Guess we'd better get some rest," said Ben.

"We don't need to complicate this with hangovers. Have you got cable up in your room?"

"Fully equipped. Watch a couple hours—it is only ten—then crash?"

"Okay by me," Les said, as they reached the elevator and Ben pushed the Up arrow. They got in and Ben pressed number five—many elevator moments to be had. The doors closed.

"Long drive all the way back to Lynnwood," said Ben, with a smirk.

"About fifteen miles I'd say, not long."

"Fifteen whole miles, and at this time of day—traffic must be really bad, huh?"

"Well, no, but parking here in the morning would be…oh, that's right, I wouldn't be parking here. Anyway, I can get up later tomorrow morning—less of a drive to BNH."

"This is a lot closer to BNH, less driving for you tomorrow."

"Much less, should take only ten, fifteen minutes."

"This was Ashley insurance, your crashing tonight, wasn't it?" asked Ben, with a grin.

"You bet."

Chapter 10

The air smelled of espionage this mid-December morning. It was the real thing; Les was a spy. The thermos of coffee and paperback were not mere props, they were equipment. The sunglasses, well, he thought he had to have 'em.

He parked as he had before near BNH; taken his time leaving The Square, so it was around eleven A.M.—the right time to get settled in for a genuine stake-out. It was the perfect time for a smoke. Les poured himself a quick cup of coffee. Half way through it, he decided to check in with his contact, so he reached into the pocket of his trenchcoat, extracted the phone, and punched the speed dial.

"Ben, Les here, everything set?"

"All set, Les," he replied, leaning on the short concrete wall at the north end of Pike Place. The flat, folded card table was leaning next to him under a couple of posters. Ben had disguised himself as a grunge local on hangout duty, and he fit in, almost invisibly well.

"Are T and A set?" Les asked, almost through the side of his mouth—like a spy not wishing detection.

"All set, Les," said Ben, making quiet emphasis on the "set."

"You've got the bottles, right?"

"What does 'all set' mean to you, Les? Does it mean, please ask me anything that you can think of, so I can stand here, looking like some asshole, saying 'all set' so many times that some passerby—who happens to hear this—will be tempted to dial 911 and have me arrested as a subversive, or some grungy crook! Everything is all set!" Ben demanded, under his breath, as he secretly glanced around to make sure that nobody near him appeared as bothered as he did.

"So, all is set then," Les concluded, and he brought his gaze up to make sure he wasn't being watched.

"I'm...going...to...kill...you!"

"All right then, I'll be in touch with you as soon as something comes up."

"Fine, Les," Ben said, "Just give me a buzz."

"Les out."

"Goodbye, Les."

Ashley and Tracy were making efficient use of the time, in their red clothes, shopping at The Place. Ashley was making use, Tracy was faking it. All had agreed that it would be unreasonable for them to stand near Ben. Two ladies wearing the same clothes, shopping together—rare, but not unheard of. Those same two ladies, hangin' with the crowd next to Victor Steinbreuk Park, would have been too weird—might have scared off the locals and exposed the team.

An hour passed; Les knew that Bateson could emerge as late as two P.M. for lunch, so he maintained his vigil. At 12:30, he decided to contact his contact—out came the cellular. He wondered how spies could have functioned in the past without them, as the speed dial shot the numbers.

"Ben?"

"Les, is he on the way?" he replied, returning from his daze.

"No, that's why I'm calling...to tell you that nothing's come up so far."

"I might have assumed that, if you simply didn't call."

"Well, I didn't want you to have to assume anything—better not to assume."

"Better really not to call if you don't have to. Talking on a cell phone destroys my cover—cracks the image I'm trying to present here."

"Okay, so then I won't phone unless there is action here at this end."

"No action, no call, right," said Ben, in mock military fashion, saluted with the phone, and folded it back into his dirty overcoat.

No other telephone incursions occurred on this Monday. Commerce at The Place went undisrupted. Ashley bought a nice red hat to go with her disguise.

*

She didn't have to clean a thing, maids did that. But she had to make sure that the maids did do it. No cooking either, unless it was for fun—she had to check on the cooks too. This was Beverly Bateson's main task, to ensure that all those jobs that she didn't have to do, were done. There were no kids. Tending to the many needs of offspring had not, and would not, tag this domestic scene. Everything was perfect—children were messy.

Mid-forties, bleached blonde, and toned. Nature had provided what plastic surgery could have. Bev was a beauty in that tight face and body, with a hint of make-up, guise of a wealthy wife. Her DNA felt comfortable in comfortable surroundings. She was Gil's, and she intended to remain so.

Beverly was scrutinizing the living room for dust when the driveway alarm gently sounded Gil's return from BNH. Front door greeting time.

"Hi, honey," Bev said, as he swung open the door, in overcoat with briefcase. He stood erect as she pecked his cheek. "Have a nice day?" she asked, in highly pitched June Cleaver.

"Fine, fine, Bev. How was your day?" he returned, as a maid removed his overcoat and took the briefcase.

"Fine, dear, fine," she replied, smiling, head tilted to the side, hands gently resting on his right wrist.

"That's good, say, I'm beat. Could you have my dinner sent up tonight, dear? Another early evening for me, I think," he said, as he patted her shoulder with his left hand and freed his other arm from her grasp.

"Certainly dear, whatever you'd like," was the sweet reply. She experienced a moment of indecision as she decided what to do with her unoccupied hands. Tough choice—she let them hang, palms up, in the tidy air. Bateson hadn't noticed, as he was making his way to the staircase, grabbing the banister for an assist on his rapid departure. He disappeared into an upper level hallway, and she continued quietly—no lips, clenched teeth, but maintaining sweetness—"Bastard!"

*

"It's a go," Les declared into the phone, hand shaking as it held the machine to his head.

"He's going out for lunch?" Ben asked, rising from his perch on the concrete wall.

"That's a roger," Les replied, eyes narrowed.

"Okay, uh, we'll set up then."

"Roger, out."

"Out, Roger," Ben said, pushed the button to disconnect, pushed again, and punched for the women.

Bateson had emerged with Matthew on this partly cloudy day, 12:15 P.M. They proceeded to the bright BMW and raced off, a few ticks above the legal speed limit. Les was on their tail, one Ford pick-up between them.

The group had decided that it would be best to set up at the first indication that Bateson might be on his way to The Place. Their theory was that the sudden appearance of a cologne stand might initially draw a crowd—novelty being a big attractant, especially for the more susceptible Christmad seasoned. The extra ten or fifteen minutes would allow the curious time to congregate and disperse. The stand would then appear as if it belonged, a better disguise, was more legit.

Ashley's phone rang. And she'd just managed to zip up the back of that pretty white dress, the one she'd seen the day before. She was in the dressing room of Fay's Fashion.

"Oh shit!" she screamed and bent down to grab her purse, grab the zipper, and grab the phone. Lisa, the sole salesperson and only other occupant of the shop besides Tracy, gave the dressing room a concerned glance and walked over to it from the register to assist. She hadn't heard the phone ring.

"Is everything all right in there?" she inquired at the swinging door. Ashley had unfolded the contraption.

"Oh, yes, I bumped an elbow, thanks," Ashley said. "I'll be fine."

"All right, Ma'am, let me…" And she was interrupted by another voice from the dressing stall.

"Hello," Ben repeated over the phone. Lisa made a puzzled expression, as she heard the strange muffled greeting, and said, "Pardon?"

"Hi, Ben. It's okay, Miss, I was also making a phone call. That was the other party answering."

Lisa replied, "Okay, Miss, well, if you need…" and back came that muffled voice.

"Hey, Ashley, what's going on?" Ben insisted, sounding very small and agitated.

"Hi, Ben, everything's fine…thanks, Miss," Ashley urged, as she began a courageous attempt to unzip the dress while maintaining phone contact with her shoulder. Lisa gave up on finishing her sentence and returned to the register, having assumed that the lady phone-addict in red had got the gist.

"It's a go, Ashley," Ben stated calmly, keeping a eye out for eaves-, street-, or sidewalk-droppers.

"Owkayphph," said Ashley.

"What?"

"Owkayphph," she repeated.

"WHAT?"

She dropped the phone while attempting to maneuver her mouth away from the speaker. Snatching it up quickly, she repeated, "Okay, we'll be right there."

"Out then," Ben retorted.

"Yes, as soon as we can," Ashley huffed, and hung up.

After carefully extracting herself from the unpurchased garment, Ashley and Tracy left Fay's, walking casual to avoid arousing suspicion. Five minutes had already passed since the alert and it would take them another casual three to reach Ben. No suspicion. Keep it cool.

They reached the grungy, poster guy and all three went about assembling the stand next to the last official one at their end of the long row. Made an odd threesome—two red-suited, Santa's helpers and one big, ugly elf. But folks didn't have much time to notice, since the team had practiced the set up, and they were good, damn good. In fact, they were arranging the white tablecloth over the erected cardtable when Ben's phone rang again; he answered, "Hello."

"It's a no go today," Les said, because their mark was headed up to Ballard, or at least not towards The Place.

Three loud, almost synchronous, "SHIT!"s could be heard at this time from three disgruntled...what...Christmas performers at the north pole of Pike Place.

*

Nylons, skirt/blouse or dress, earrings—the whole nine yards—Beverly was always dressed for dinner, though busy checking on things during the final moments of his evening return. She had to take it easy so as not to take on too much of a glow—being all sweaty would spoil the effect. "The effect" maintained the current lifestyle. She'd completed her inspection of some of their top-shelf, name-dropper artwork—that she neither admired, comprehended, nor trusted—when the gong sounded. Her countenance perked up as she made a final, personal reflection inspection.

"Hi, honey," she said, as he opened the door. A perky peck and she asked, "Have a nice day?"

"Fine, fine, Bev. How was your day?" he replied, the maid experiencing deja vu with his overcoat and briefcase.

"Fine, dear, fine," was the reply, his wrist locked onto with a smile from tilted head.

"That's good, say, I'm beat. Could you have my dinner sent up, dear? Another early evening for me, I think," shoulder pat, arm freed, and headed for the gate.

"Certainly dear, whatever you'd like," said sweetly, her hands descending to her thighs. Up the stairs he fled. "Asshole."

*

"How about this one?" Ashley asked, holding a blue blouse to her chest.

"Fine, they're all fine," answered Tracy, in hopes of some break in the interrogation. Shopping had gone from passable to painful for her. Ashley was enjoying.

"And this? This versus the last?" Ashley continued, with a brown. They were conducting this survey in Cathy's Concepts.

"Oh, you know, they're both so gorgeous that I can't make up my mind," she replied, feigning mock sincerity.

"A little help here, Tracy; this is important!"

"I think red's your color."

"Red! Okay, if you don't want to help just say so, okay, Tracy? Just say so."

"Ashley, I..." and the cellular buzzed. She slammed the blouse back on the rack and fumbled for the phone.

"Hello," she said.

"The dog is off the leash," Ben said.

"What?"

"The horse is out the gate."

"What?"

"He's on his way, get up here."

"Well, why the fu…why didn't you say so, dammit?" Ashley said, frowning. Tracy and Greta, the salesperson, were beginning to also.

"Bored, I guess," he confessed.

"Well, get bored on your own damn time! Jesus! We'll be right up," she snapped, collapsed her phone, and to Greta said, "Friend's having a baby—broke water, gotta go. Thanks for everything."

And the two made their casual exit.

*

A mid-thirties couple approached Tracy and Ashley, as they stood behind the cologne stand.

"Come on, Julius, it says Yule Musk—sounds Christmassy," his wife said, hugging his left arm.

"Definite Christmas sound to it, where's it come from? Seen it before, Vicky?"

They were still on approach—three meters, and counting. Tracy and Ashley were keeping the tablecloth down and neat between wind gusts.

"Well, no, I haven't seen it. It must be new."

"Doesn't come from reindeer, does it?"

"No, I doubt it. Try some."

"Oh, all right, I'll give it a shot."

"He'd like to try some, please," said Vicky to Tracy.

"Certainly," Tracy replied, as she held one of the smaller, bottles. "Could you bring your face a little closer please, sir?"

Julius leaned a bit over the table, providing the needed close-up, and Tracy misted him in the face with the advertised Yule Musk—it said

Yule Musk in big letters on a banner taped to the tablecloth on the exposed side.

Vicky sniffed his neck and complained, "I don't smell anything," to his right ear, and then to the marketers, "I don't smell anything."

Julius took a gentle swipe of his cheek and smelled his hand, "I don't either, Vicky, not a whiff."

Ashley answered, "Yule Musk is a relatively new type of cologne, one of a recent variety, recently developed. It is odorless when applied—after some time, after reacting chemically with naturally produced body secretions, the final scent is formed. And…and…only women can smell it. Detectable only by women," Ashley pronounced proudly, holding her product up under her chin with both hands.

"Getting anything yet, dear?" Julius inquired of his wife, directing his cheek her way.

"Nothing yet, honey," she replied, hopefully. "Thank you very much," she said to the Yule Muskateers, "Let's go, Julius, I'm getting a chill." And she nudged him back on course, towards the fresh fish.

As they walked out of range, Tracy said, "Nice touch. This sounds like a really interesting product."

"It is. Believe in it!" insisted Ashley, and sprayed Tracy on the nose. Tracy returned fire, and her peripheral sensors picked up a sudden motion by Ben on her right. He was signaling with a waving arm—Bateson was coming their way.

"Here he comes," she said; Ashley nodded and moved to the other side of the stand—small bottle in one, bottle of Greed Stopper in the other hand.

"That Japanese place might have some. Why the hell do you have to eat Tofu anyway, Reg? You sick or something?"

"Soy protein consumption may reduce risk of heart disease," Reginald insisted, walking in step with his boss. And smartly dressed.

"Guy like you worried about heart disease? You haven't got an ounce of fat on you!" Gil said, stopping for a visual confirmation of this statement, gauging with his outstretched arms.

"Because I try to eat right, Gil…and get proper exercise," he replied, also having stopped, to allow for the visual confirmation.

"Well, good for you, Reg, good for you," stated Gil, having resumed forward motion. They passed Ben, who was leaning on the wall, and proceeded south. Ashley made an abrupt tactical maneuver and tactically jumped in front of the two—deploying her liquid ordnance to each face, point blank. Small bottle for the smartly dressed guy and large bottle for Bateson.

"This is Yule Musk," she announced, almost breathlessly, "a brand new product for the Holiday season."

Gil was thrown off guard. "What the hell? I didn't ask for any Yule Musk!" he demanded.

Reginald was behind him, both hands aflutter, in a fruitless attempt to fan off the musk.

"And I don't smell anything. What is this, fake Yule Musk?" Bateson asked, agitated.

"No, sir, it is only detectable by women, and only after some time on the body," returned Ashley, making musky eye contact. Bateson reacted with a slight grin, tilt of the head, and a narrowing of the eyes—he'd also liked the word, "body."

"I hope this doesn't clash with the cologne I've got on," Reginald warned Ashley. "How do you get off assaulting people with odorless musk without their permission? I mean, is this legal?" Before Ashley could respond—she was a lawyer—Gil interjected, again demonstrating that chivalry wasn't completely in the toilet.

"It's done all the time, Reg, relax; it won't confuse your cologne, or whatever the damn phrase is." He smiled at Ashley, took her hand in his, and said, "Don't worry, he won't sue you. I'm his boss, I'll fire him if he tries."

"Oh, thank you, sir, thank you," said Ashley, with sincere gratitude and an elfish glint in her eye. Tracy was sincerely grateful, from the other side of the stand.

"And Merry Christmas," she called out, as they left in search of soy.

"Mission accomplished!" Ben said casually into his phone, scratching his side with the other hand.

"Darlene, look here—free samples," Herbert said to his burly wife.

"No, Herbert, you don't need no—what's it called—Yule Musk on ya! You already smell," she said, eyeing him top to bottom.

"Oh, come on dear, it'll be fun," coaxed Herbert, grabbing the upper arm nearest him and hugging it with his cheek.

The women were in the process of destanding—banner was hanging from one end, barely legible; bottles rattling on the half bare table, as they began to fold up the cloth.

"Okay, Herbert, if you want to. I guess it's okay," she consented, as they reached the crippled display.

"I'd like to try some of your Yule Musk," Herbert announced to Tracy, who turned to Ashley for advice.

"I'm sorry, sir, we're winding this operation down," Ashley snapped.

"But I've never tried any Yule Musk," pleaded Herbert.

"Well, sorry, this stuff's gone sour—we've got to replenish our stock. Going back to the ranch right now, got to squeegee off some more reindeer sweat," stated Ashley in earnest.

"EEUUWW!" squealed Herbert. "EEUUWW!"

"Come on, Herbert," Darlene commanded, grasping him by the shoulders and pointing him down the aisle, "You're not smellin' like some damned reindeer!"

Chapter 11

Les drove the exhausted Greed Team down to Sea-Tac; they made their flight arrangements—snagging some rides on the several daily commuter flights down Golden State way— and had a couple of social hours before taking off. Ben and Tracy caught earlier flights, leaving Ashley alone with Les for about an hour. They sat by her gate in those highly ergonomic plastic seats, drinking enormous coffee.

"You were great out there today, Les," declared Ashley, with pupils most dilated.

"I've heard that one before," he quipped, amazed at how teenage he could be when his emotions were on the fringe.

"Do you think we've done the right thing? I mean, you don't think we've done a bad thing, do you?" she asked.

"Bad? Probably not. No, I don't think so. But we are crazy," he said, hoping to convince himself that they hadn't done wrong, exactly.

"Plain nuts…loco," Ashley piped in, with a protracted "l," "…locomotive!"

Les smiled broadly, relieved by the change of track. "Love locomotion," he let slip, but also with protracted "l"'s. They let these last words hang in the air for a moment. Les in regret; Ashley, well, who was to know?

Time passed while Les wondered how they would choreograph that final parting. Wave, handshake, quick hug, full-body contact grapple, mutual kiss on the lips, or that deeply gratifying, deep in the mouth, tongue twist.

They opted for somewhere between a hug and a grapple before Ashley got her ticket stubbed at the ramp.

*

Gil was proud of the rock wall surrounding the grounds; opened his gate with a touch of a button. Long driveway, big trees, shrubs—nicely trimmed. Gil was proud of the way his gardeners trimmed his shrubs. He couldn't hear it as he tripped the sensor on his approach to the big stone house, alarming Beverly of his arrival. Gil was proud of the big stone house too.

"Hi, honey," she said as he entered. One quick peck and she asked, "Have a nice day?"

"Fine, ff..." he paused, and gazed at her; gave her a small smile, "fine, Bev. How was your day?" he said, the maid pausing to glimpse at the Mrs. before she helped him off with the coat and briefcase.

Beverly caught her breath and managed a somewhat choked, "Fine, dear, fine," then she didn't know what the hell to do. Hold the wrist? Hold a hand? This wasn't in the damned script! She defaulted to hands at side and smile with tilted head.

"That's good, Beverly. Say, you know, I'm beat. Could you have my dinner sent up, dear? Another early evening for me, I think," he said, as he remembered her shoulder and noticed his free arm before heading toward the staircase.

"Certainly, dear, whatever you'd like," was her line. He ascended. "Shithead."

*

One week following The Treatment, Steve was still on the job, in his cubicle, engineering. But the air was thick with anticipation. He wouldn't see the results directly, but they would trickle down. If they were to…He didn't know; this was an experiment. One gigantic rat—a rat, who happened to sign the paycheck. Be a far stretch to make the connection though, he had been at work. Steve was clear. Ben had told him that they wouldn't be able to find the virus anyway. So everything was copacetic. Steve wondered where "copacetic" had come from. He didn't recall ever knowing the word. It was the cubicles. The damned cubicles. The damned layoffs! Jesus!

"Good morning, Steve," said Fred Gompers, in his short, wide, bald way.

"Morning, Fred," and he let the usual "what's up" hang in silence. There was anticipation in the air that didn't need any more of a crowd. If any news was to come down, this man was the wide conduit—the General Manager of MPG.

"Got the word from above."

"Word?"

"Yep. Good news, Steve, no layoffs. Downsizing has been downsized. You, or rather, we, have no worries."

"That's fantastic," Steve almost shouted; it had been too loud for cubicle space, so he got a mental hold of himself, and continued, "What happened?"

"I don't know, Steve, don't know. Just got the memo from Human Resources; Bob Pridgeon must have been told to tell what's his name—oh, I can't…the head of Resources—to lighten up on the layoffs," he answered, tucking his thumbs under his belt, and rocking as he stood.

"No layoffs? It's been a while. Feels kinda strange not having a layoff hanging over your head, you know?"

"Well, I don't have it hanging over me as much as you do—being higher up in the eschalon—but I do know what you mean."

"Can you think of any reason why all of a sudden we're not downsizing?"

"No, I can't really. Maybe we're making too damn much money."

"Yeah, right."

"Let me put it this way, maybe now simply isn't an appropriate time for them to get nasty in the market. You know, they're sitting tight—sit and wait. Holdin' their own."

"Okay! Fine by me."

"Fine with me too. Do you think I like going around all the time with crappy news? No, sir…no, sir."

"I know that, Fred, not your fault, it's business.

"Business."

That's right, just business."

CHAPTER 12

People talked about the constant rain in the Northwest. It happened. The Core Group was walled in dark mahogany again. All were seated except the CEO—his status made him never late. But this time the usual atmospheric charge was absent from his entrance.

"Gentlemen, it's only a few days into the new year, new century for that matter. I don't know whether it's the new millennium or not, but what the hell anyway. So what's that make us?" he asked, seating himself at the head before they replied, without even a glance at them as they gave their enthusiastic response. The tone wasn't there. The usual kickass, fuck you sound of Gil's opener came off limp.

"Big 'N Hard!" was stated, not very well orchestrated—vastly out of synch. An afterthought. Bateson didn't seem to notice. Reginald needed a reasonable explanation, and quick—this bothered him very much.

"Are you feeling okay, sir?" he asked, with genuine concern in his small eyes.

"Fine, Reg…I mean Reginald, fine," Gil said, without that shit eatin' smirk that all had grown so fond of. But a pleasant smile, Reginald's nervous quotient went through the roof.

"That's good, Gil," offered Reg, unconvincingly.

"Thank you. Now, how are we doing?" Bateson asked the room. "Bob, how are you doing?"

"I'm doing fine, Gil. How are you?" asked the CFO, caught off guard, off his chair.

"Like I said, Bob, fine. How're we doing financially, Bob?" Gil asked, eyes lackluster.

"Great, great. No complaints. Wouldn't touch a thing," he said, as simply as he could.

"Positive cash flow, margins rising—got a little to play around with, do we, Bob?"

"Depends on what you mean by play, but, yes, we're in a good, solid position right now," Bob stated, having emphasized the "good, solid" with delicate, open-hand karate chops to the table.

"That's what I wanted to hear. Reg...inald, let's hear from your department."

"Thank you. Yes, everything here seems to be fine, as well," he said, still uncertain of the boss, still exercising extreme caution.

"Mind elaborating a bit for us?"

"Yes, well, work is progressing on the new line of faster chips—somewhere near two gigahertz. Should be through with testing in a month," said the edgy Tech and Manufacturing, well-dressed, Senior Vice President and General Manager.

"On schedule, are we, Reginald?" Gil responded, not even slightly proud of himself at having mastered this employee's proper address—it was now on autopilot.

"Yes, I would say that we are, indeed, on schedule," he gently concluded, careful not to tip the old fart out of whatever mindframe he was perched in. Reginald also didn't catch the proper address finally landing on him.

"Susan, my dear, what have you to tell us?"

"My dear? Oh, how sweet of you, Gil," she said, as she rose in her chair removing that question about osteoporosis. "Our commercial has really caught on, even though it isn't soccer season...I think. Anyway, it's been a "GOAL" with many of the Hispanics, and surprisingly, other ethnic groups too. WASP's like to hear "GOAL" a lot, apparently."

"They like the sound of a score, something like that?" Gil offered.

"Something like that, I guess. Anyway, aside from that, as soon as Matthew gets finished with re-organizing our new acquisitions, we'll be tackling that. We're in good shape."

"Good shape?"

"Good shape. Lookin' good," she replied, exhaling audibly and resuming her usual slump.

"Thank you, Susan, thank you," said Gil, with marked calm. He slowly turned his head from her to the final VP and ever so quietly said, "Matthew, how are things with CBD?"

This really threw him off his stump. He knew that they often put up with his "challenges," but he didn't deserve this mocking. A sense of humor was a useful social tool, but this went beyond simple jocularity—this was plain cruel! Nasty and cruel! Matthew worked up an incredible stammer.

"Fuh, fuh, fuh…fuh, fuh fuh," he began. The other three senior VP's had been thinking along the same lines and so were fully prepared—and were actually hoping for—a good, solid, "FUCK YOU!"

"Fuh, fuh, fuh…" he continued, very wide-eyed, red-faced, head fully extended on straining neck—it had to pop! And did, "For your inform ma, ma, ma…mation, I'm not a cripple! I'm na, na, na…not a nutcase! Give me some respect!"

"Of course, you have my respect, Matthew!" This full name, Gil had conquered also. "What did I say?" he asked, not knowing how utterly callous he'd been.

"Treat me like a child," accused Matthew, wishing he hadn't put it that way, but glad for having been able to put something out in its entirety without a skip.

"Matthew, I did not intend to treat you in any manner, but with complete respect. You do excellent work!" said the CEO, with complete conviction.

"Okay, then," Matthew said, still amazed at himself, "okay, let's see. Yes, I'm eyeing a company that is heavy into video conferencing called, Icy You. Not a big firm—got a lot of potential—I think it would be friendly."

"Friendly, huh?"

"Yes, friendly."

"Take a lot of cash?"

"A fair amount," Matthew replied, engine warm, in high gear.

"Fine job, Matthew, wonderful. But you know, folks?" and he paused to let some air out, "I sort of feel it's time to step back and take a gander at the big picture. Lean back, mentally, and take a good, long look at where we're headed and how we're gonna get there," Bateson said, as he slid down on his seat and folded his hands behind his head, gazing up at the ceiling tiles and ornate hanging lamp. He'd forgotten about doing it "mentally."

During the quiet moments that followed, the "mental" space around them was pounded with confusion and frustration and many other bad things. He'd never acted this way before! Was he on something? Lose a cherished relative or friend? No, he was not one to cherish! Jesus! What'll happen to all my BNH stock? Shit! Goddamn him! None of them knew who was thinking what, but the gist of their silent facial expressions revealed them to be in general agreement, "That bastard!" Unless he doesn't mean what we think he's saying.

"You know, we've got some fine workers here at Big 'N Hard, and I've been feeling lately like it's about time we threw them a bone, a little extra something, you know?" he stated, and stared into their frozen scowls. None dared speak.

"So, Matthew, I think we'll hold back on this takeover idea for the moment, maintain a decent cash reserve. Bob, I want you to get together with Reginald and whoever, or is it whomever, anyway, guy down in Human Resources, other folks…I want to hire—full time, full benefits—any temp who has been with us more than two years." The "mental" space was starting to quiver and quake. "We need to hold on to loyal, hard-working employees. Aside from that, I want to give those workers who've been with us, oh, say at least seven years, a bonus—call it a loyalty thing. Say two, no, five percent of salary. Got to keep a hold of the good ones. That's all; that's about it, I'd say. Fairly simple, not too dramatic. But…a nice gesture. What do you think?" he inquired of the room.

The room was not happy. If the walls had mouths…Traffic in that "mental" space was as congested as it had been—lots of air rage—but then on the horizon it appeared. Faint at first, it grew wider and brighter—the thought, the idea, the conclusion—well, it went, "Could have been a whole helluva lot worse!"

"Sounds good to me, Gil," Bob said, forced smile.

"All right! Give our loyal dogs a bone, fine by me," Susan declared, glazed eyes.

"Yep," sputtered Matthew.

"I think that's a wise move, Gil, wise move," stated Reginald, with head shaking "no."

"Fine then, fine. Let's see some results. I believe this a positive step for BNH. Not only will it improve employee relations—that's the most important—but, who knows, it might even increase productivity. Who knows? Anyway, I think that's enough for this meeting. Anyone got anything else to add?"

"No, I'm good," replied Bob.

"That's fine," said Reginald.

"Okay by me, Gil," added Susan.

"Nope," Matthew managed.

"All right then," Bateson concluded. "Oh, I almost forgot. What are we?"

The Group seemed puzzled for a second, glanced at each other in puzzling ways the next, had a sudden collective realization, and said—after the delay, but almost in unison—"Big 'N Hard!"

*

Steve and co-engineer, Irwin Frink, liked smoking stogies while they were shooting. Away from electronic reality for those thirty minutes, it was getting to be routine—a mid-morning half hour break in the new smoking lounge; three days felt as if they'd always done it. They stunk afterwards, but the cubicles didn't prevent them from airing out.

"Wonder if this new management, or whatever they're doing, might extend this to forty-five," the short, gnarled, next cubicle neighbor of Steve said.

"Be nice, but how far do you think this new good guy policy can go? It's got to start cutting too deep into their profits; top management's not going to take a hit," replied Steve, talking around his gar, eyeballing his next shot.

"They might," said Irwin, optimistically, as he stood to the side with his cue vertically inclined.

"Dream on."

"They've done all this other stuff lately, who would've expected? They've been acting weird—taking a pay cut wouldn't be too out of line of acting weird."

"Could be, Irwin, could be. I'm not complaining."

"Me neither, but you know, Steve, I think they may be onto something. I feel better after these extended breaks. I think I get more work done—my productivity has increased as a result."

"That sort of happened to me too—eight in the side," Steve said, and Irwin acknowledged his intentions with a nod. In the side it went.

"Good game," said Irwin, "got time for another?"

"We can go until it's time; we have another ten, I think," Steve replied, and checked his watch. "Yep, ten."

"Okay, you break," Irwin declared, as he racked the balls.

Fred Gompers entered the room with a broad, face-splitting grin and asked, "Steve, could I speak with you for a minute in the hall?"

"Sure, let me set this gar down," said Steve, as he placed it in the tray on the coffee table and followed Fred out the door.

"Didn't want to say this in front of Irwin, he hasn't got enough seniority. Steve, you're getting a five percent bonus, tomorrow or the next day," said Fred, extending his hand for a shake.

Steve shook and said, "Wow, this is all right. What's going on around here, Fred? First all that upgrading of the temps to full-time, then this break thing with new rooms and all that…now this. I'd say pinch me, but I don't do that."

"Listen, I'm not absolutely positive, but I heard—now mind you, this is only hearsay, it's only a rumor—but word's going round that Bateson's changed; found religion or something. No one knows for sure, but these new decisions are originating from him," Fred advised, but quietly.

"Senior VP's aren't putting their two cents in?"

"Not at all. In fact, they're against all of these changes. Not to Bateson's face, but they're talking. Wouldn't be surprised if some of them jumped ship, if this kind of stuff continues," said Fred, shakin his head and staring at the air.

"So we get a little turnover at the top, what's the big deal? We get some new management," Steve said with a baffled expression, resting his hands on the upright cue.

"Maybe it would be no big deal. Bateson's the brains behind this operation. He founded BNH in a bathtub or something like that," stated Fred, smiling.

"I think it was his parents' garage with two matchsticks," corrected Steve, as he entered the fray of weak humor.

"On top of the garage, in a tent during a rainstorm with an erector set."

"No, under the garage with a flashlight and some girly magazines!"

"Oh, hell, well, you got your bonus," concluded Fred, with a pat to Steve's back, as he began his way down the hall.

"Thanks for letting me know, you made my day," said Steve to Fred's back. He raised an arm to signal Steve, "You're welcome."

*

The house on a cul-de-sac in Tukwila was one of dozens of very box-like, very small-yarded, very new, very expensive, Cape Codesque residences. Steve had been in awe when he discovered how little he could get for so much. Debt was the fashion of the late 90's—his family's contribution to the strong U.S. economy, about to set a record for duration of sustained growth. True patriots, the Williams.

The smart, 90's developer had really packed 'em in, but in a deceptively attractive way—using greenbelts. Kept a narrow band of the original forest—firs and cedars plus ground cover—on the outer perimeter of the cul-de-sac, so it appeared to the residents as if they inhabited an island in the woods. Because they couldn't clearly see the million other self-deluded islands that had them surrounded. But appearance over reality was very 90's for Hamster Wheelers. Steve had gotten off the wheel and was starting to rattle the cage, perhaps.

He parked his Legacy Outback—sensibly priced with all-wheel drive, in case of one of those rare snows. Out of the car, one of those "What a great day" stretches, and it was into his domain he went.

Rebecca, his wife, was in the sunken living room to the left of the entrance, playing blocks with their two year-old boy and three year-old girl.

Steve stopped and stared. Freeze-frame—perfect domestic bliss, a picture. Made it all worthwhile—reason for putting up with all the chips.

His wife rose to her average height of around five foot five to greet her tall husband with a hug.

"I got some interesting news today, honey," whispered Steve into her right ear. He was bent over at the waist.

"What is it, Steve?" she asked, pulling away to meet his eyes with hers.

"I got a five percent bonus," he said, finishing it off with a quiet laugh, huge set of teeth on display.

"Oh, that's fantastic. God, that's great," she squeezed, gently.

*

He had some information—what was it referred to as in the espionage game—anyway, he had it. Steve felt the need to share this material with his fellow Greed Teammates. The point man was Ashley. He punched her number that same evening.

"Hello," said Ashley.

"Hello, Ashley, this is Steve. How are you doing?"

"Steve, hi, fine, and you?"

"Very fine! Really very fine!"

"Really very fine?"

"Yes, really very fine."

"So, something's happened, I presume. And it's good, this thing that's happened."

"Oh, it's good."

"It's good?"

"Very good."

"Well, we could go on like this. It is fun. Somewhat mysterious, that sort of thing. But could you tell me what the hell happened?"

And he the hell did. Ashley decided that it would be strategic to meet in San Francisco in two weeks—no more, no less—for some reason or reasons only she knew. It didn't matter to Steve. But the others, the others would have to be convinced—this was what Ashley was determined to do.

*

A familiar route for Gil this was; he went there one or two times a week for lunch. On this day the drive wasn't the same, wasn't filled with the same routine anticipation; this time was kind of sad. He was going to break it off—let her down easy. Same street, same condo with a view—a heavy view this time. He knocked on the door.

"Gil, honey, nice to see you," Dolly said, big hair in place, wearing a white robe—neck lined with fluff. She grabbed his body in her arms, reached up, and clamped her lips onto his.

"Dolly, sweety," he said, once he'd freed his mouthparts, "it's nice to see you too." They backed into the place as a single unit—part of normal courtship ritual—and closed the door.

"Be just a minute, hon," she said, as she released him and sauntered into the bathroom.

Bateson caught his breath. "But sweety, I…" and before he could go on, she was behind the closed door, setting up.

This one-bedroom was a tribute to wild, dead cats. Leopards and tigers mostly, maybe a jaguar or two—a few of them actual skins. Bedspread, pillow cases, wall-hangings, rug, some prints—it was a wonder. Gil didn't mind, hadn't…now it mattered even less; at least they made her happy. Dolly emerged with even wilder, bigger hair wearing tassels over her big, bare-breasted nipples, a leopard print thong bikini with snaps for quick removal, and high heels. She turned on the stereo and the show started—bump and grind, bass and drums. Gil was smiling, but shaking his head. He gestured "no, no, no," with his hands, which she interpreted as meaning something like, "Today I'm an inexperienced teenage boy—first time with a hooker—please be gentle, but very obvious…you lead." When what he really meant was, "Not today.

Not ever again." He decided a verbal signal might improve the picture.

"NO. NOT TODAY," he insisted over the music. She turned off the stereo, looking startled—tassels stopped twirling.

"What's the matter, honey, you don't like the leopard? No tassels today?" she asked, voice pitched to the ceiling.

"Dolly...Dolly, that's why I came here today, to tell you something," he said with sad eyes.

"Tell me something? Now? We don't usually talk 'til after. You want to talk first?"

"Yeah, sweety, let's talk first. You have a seat there," he said, indicating the bed, "and I'll tell you what's been on my mind lately."

"On your mind?" she asked, sincerely struggling with this script change.

"Dolly, I've been thinking...no...feeling mostly, that this thing isn't going anywhere. You know? Sure, we have a good time, fantastic time, all this cat stuff and everything, but it's not the right thing for us, Dolly. Not right. You deserve to have a good, solid relationship. You need to find yourself a real man; you deserve a real man. And I, I need to commit to my dear wife. I owe her that," said Gil, staring down at the deceased feline under his feet.

"But Gil, I want you," she pleaded, with earnest pout.

"You're simply not going to get me. I am not going to divorce Beverly to marry you. You know that," he said, with gaze raised all the way up to her kneecaps, unable to meet her disappointed visage.

"Oh, I know that. But what we got here is perfect. Perfect for me, perfect for you."

"Not perfect, Doll, not perfect. For those same reasons I mentioned."

"Aw, come on. I know, you just need to see some nippies," she said, as she whipped off the tassels.

"NO!" he shouted, regained composure, and continued calmly, "no, it's nothing like that."

He paused and she covered her breasts in thought.

"Now, Dolly, it's over. But I'm not going to leave you out in the cold. And put a top on or something, will you?" said Gil, shaking his head with a downturned mouth. She reached for a bra hanging on a bedpost.

"Not out in the cold?" Dolly asked, perking up a perk or two.

"Not out in the cold. I'll send you a monthly check; don't want to send cash in the mail—let my accountant deal with it, a business expense or something. Anyway, you'll still have this place and plenty of spending money," he assured her.

"Okay, if this will really make you feel better, I guess it'll have to do. You're breaking my heart, you know, but if this is what you want, this is what you'll get," she concluded, with unknown lucidity.

"Well…hey…glad you understand," Gil said, wondering who had said that, "um, well, I guess that's it then," and finished this with a palms up "who woulda thought?"

"I guess you're right, Gil, this is the best for the both of us," she said, rising to arm him across the shoulders and escort him to the door. "Can I expect a check fairly soon? I'm running kind of short at the moment."

"I'll have one sent tomorrow."

"That's great, Gil," Dolly replied, with all her teeth, and opened the door.

Bateson returned to his car, glowing with good feeling. It was nice to feel good. Damn nice.

Chapter 13

"Every third commercial, there's some shill with an English or Australian accent," said Tracy, disgusted.

"Something like, hey, if one of those Brits likes it, then it must be first rate. Bastards," agreed Ashley, somewhat, to Tracy's titter and what verged on a belly-laugh from Les overacting.

"And some are so obviously fake. 'Hey, you, hear my obviously fake English accent? Well, then, buy this car, mate!'," mocked Tracy.

"That's been going on for a long time though," said Les, regaining some dignity, at least in his mind. The three were sitting at a sea lion-side table in that restaurant at The Pier having coffee. Steve and Ben were off on a walk to Marina Green.

"Do you guys ever watch football?" Tracy continued.

"Yeah," "Sure."

"You know all the garbage the color guy gives you about what a solid citizen—family man, role model, charity giver, old lady across the street walker—each of the players is?" she asked, profoundly disturbed by this deception.

"Makes me sick," admitted Ashley, joining Tracy in her sentiments.

"I laugh," Les said, "it's all too unreal. This is the way the world works these days."

"Les," Ashley stated, dismayed, "for a smart guy, you can sure be obtuse at times."

"Obtuse?"

"Yeah, obtuse."

"Maybe so, but refresh my memory, what does obtuse mean?" asked Les, wound opening.

"Obtuse, stupid, dim-witted..."

"Okay, I get it," he interrupted, each successive word, added insult.

"You can't accept the world the way it presents itself—you don't laugh it off, you act, you do something!" Ashley scolded.

"Sorry for being so bathetic," Les replied, accenting it with mock schoolboy.

"You write the show's producers—I haven't ever, but someone could. You stop watching football, or all so-called professional sports, for that matter."

"Yeah, you're right, I shouldn't sit around like some maniac, laughing at all the incredible insults the world features on today's listings. It all seems so futile. What can one person really do?" Les said, regaining lost territory.

"This is getting kind of heavy, don't you think?" asked Tracy. "I mean, we are only talking about football and TV, aren't we? Sure there's the big picture, but we are just talking about TV."

"You're right, Tracy," Ashley said, "we can save this kind of discussion for the real thing, something that really matters—our experiment."

"Okay, save it for later. Back to TV...you know, here's something else that really bugs me. Remember the WTO riots up in Seattle recently? Got huge coverage on the local stations. So there I am, sitting in front of the tube, trying to watch some nice, decent, holiday rioting, and the newscaster can't seem to shut the hell up!" exclaimed Les, worked up a couple of notches.

"Kind of distracting, huh?" quipped Ashley.

"Well, jeez, you want to be able to hear the action—an armchair rioter wants to get the real feel of the melee."

"Newscasters seem to feel the need to fill a void. That void being any time they're not crowding the air with their blather," said Ashley.

"And the repetition. Over and over and over, the same bullshit!" said Les, taking it up another notch.

"And they reuse the same damned footage several times that same day," injected Tracy.

"It's shameless," stated Ashley, hint of a smile.

"I think I'll go out and bark about it with those sea lions," declared Les, sharing in the easing.

"I'm not going to watch any riots for a while," announced Tracy, resolute.

"You do that, Tracy," agreed Ashley, with some serious nonsense on her face.

"You can bet I will," Tracy smirked, finally.

The hikers returned and they switched to wine. Ashley had decided that they should complete their business early on this weekender, so they could enjoy some Bay Area for at least a half day. There weren't any minutes to read—though they'd agreed that formality was useful in principle, it was not regulation. Ashley asked Steve to give them an update; this was sufficient organization.

He relayed all the uplifting, upsizing news—the raises, the bonuses, the mid-morning breaks; the temps realizing a less transient status—the new stuff. And it was good. Then came the unconfirmed, the innuendo, the rumor mongering.

"But," Steve continued, "word is spreading that senior management is not at all happy with the changes. Gompers, the GM of my group, is saying that some of them are starting to make inquiries with other companies. He says to keep an eye on the stock price, sell if it starts to drop. I don't know, I will watch the market, but I can't see how losing a few management figure heads is going to affect the company's worth."

"Price often reflects perception of worth—like ninety-nine percent of the e-stocks," stated Ashley.

Les could feel something stroking his left leg under the table. The red-haired, financial advisor was seated to his left. He dared not check, in case that'd be a stroke-stopper. So, he smiled and stared straight ahead at the air over Ben.

"I've got a lot of money in those stocks, so if it takes a downturn…"

"May go down in the short run; may be a buying opportunity, it depends on what you think the company can do in the long run," Ashley advised.

Ben began to wonder about the *stupid* that was making itself known on Les's face. He opted to take time to gather more data—could have been just the wine smirking.

"All in all, though," Steve said, "it seems like the stuff worked. Bateson—according to everyone in the know—has changed; he is less tight-fisted. The senior VP shits who surround him wouldn't have initiated these changes. It's Bateson, he's lost his greed."

Ben was proud, it was his Greed Stopper that had done it. Ashley was proud, she'd been the point man. Tracy was glad; at least they hadn't been talking about her life. Les was still getting stroked.

After dinner, the others decided to make it an early evening so they'd be fresh for Sunday. Ben and Les, still clinging to a strict college tradition, decided to do some moderate pounding—some tapping? In any case, they ordered a pitcher of microbrew—though in such quantity, the term "micro" didn't really seem appropriate. So, they went on to test current beer theory to see whether the stuff improved their friendship or proved the opposite.

"What were you grinning about? You had this stupid smile on your face all evening," said Ben.

"Nothing really, glad that the experiment was working, I guess."

"It wasn't that kind of expression. Your face was not saying, 'Gee, isn't it wonderful that our experiment is working!' No, it was saying something more clever, something more sly."

"I haven't got that much control over the way my face appears; I was just feeling good."

"Don't lie to me! It was Ashley, wasn't it. You've got something going with Ashley, haven't you."

"Nope, I wish, but nothing is going on right now," Les insisted.

"Don't lie to me, asshole," exclaimed Ben, proving the theory—at least providing supporting evidence.

"What the fuck? Calling me an asshole? What got your shorts in a knot?" replied Les, also in line with the theoretical beer story.

Ben scanned the nearby tables for observers. They were watching.

Quietly, Ben said, "Okay, let's be honest, we're both fuckin' hot for Ashley, right? I want to know if you've got something going—then I'll back off."

"You don't sound like you're backing off—more like pissing off," said Les, quietly, forcing those close by to be at even quieter tables, with very strained, craned necks.

"You seem pretty calm about all of this. You're hiding something. There is something going on. And right behind my back!" blurted Ben, extending the audible range.

"Yeah, fuck, right behind your fuckin' back. I'm humpin' Ashley, and all you've got to do is turn around to get an eyeful," said Les, bringing in more audience participation.

"I thought so, you fuckin' bastard! I thought we were friends," Ben replied, emphasizing his statement with a half-mug guzzle.

"I'm not humpin' Ashley," admitted Les, to many disappointed faces. "And even if I were, it wouldn't be against you, or whatever. She's not yours."

"But you know I like her."

"Grow the fuck up."

"You fuckin' grow the fuck up."

The evening's pounding soon ceased.

*

Rented bikes in The Park. Golden Gate never seemed crowded. There always seemed to be some open space to spread your tires and catch so much beauty in so little time—caught up in the momentum. Mountain bikes, some thought the finest invention since...well, another damn fine invention. There weren't many steep ones for testing these hill-climbing wonders in The Park, but it was still reassuring to know that any grade could be conquered. Picnic on a huge patch of lawn, all to themselves.

"Being a park ranger would be nice," mused Tracy, as they sat on the grass in a circle with their deli.

"Do they have rangers here? Aren't there only groundskeepers?" asked Les.

"I don't know," replied Steve.

"Me neither," Ben said, as he bunched up the sandwich wrapper and placed it in his fannypack. He got up, walked from the group about fifteen feet, and performed a handstand.

"You're real talented, Ben," noted Ashley, with a grin. Ben was still standing.

"How long can you go?" asked Tracy, impressed in a way similar to Ashley.

"I don't know," grunted Ben.

"Bet he can last a long time," quipped Ashley.

"Yeah...real long," agreed Tracy.

Les had been simply watching these festivities when at last he decided to make a move of his own, "Ashley, would you like to take a ride to Ocean Beach?"

"Okay, that sounds like fun," she replied cheerfully. Tracy and Steve remained silent. Ben was caught with his pants upside down. They left. Ben was still standing.

The waves. Was it a roar, a crash...anyway, the loud sound and vibration on the sand seemed to crowd out all thought. Ashley and Les thoughtlessly walked their borrowed bikes across the beach to the surf, feeling the cool air.

They stopped on some sand just out of wave reach and paused. Without a thought. Ashley gazed over at his silhouette, steadily, until he turned to meet her eyes. She bent forward and kissed him long and sweet—lips only. A wave caught them.

Chapter 14

Flooding the room with full-spectrum light with bright colors on the walls would have been cheery. If it were a mahogany day, the windows would be leaking some rainy day light—a somber backdrop for the Core Group. As the days before had been, without regard to the weather.

Bateson walked in like he was wearing a big Hawaiian hat and a flowered shirt—none dared look farther south. Gil had this big, Poi-eatin' grin on his face.

"Good afternoon, all," he announced, seating himself at the head.

"Afternoon," "Hello," "Good day," and "Hi" came back at him.

"So, here we are again," he remarked, placing first his elbows on the table, then chin on the knuckle perch. "Who are we?"

"A computer hardware manufacturer," offered Reginald—middle seat, front row, slicked hair neatly parted and combed to the side. There was a pause, giving Reg some time to adopt a frown—having realized that he'd missed the point completely. Even though that had been Bateson's lamest opening for a BNH Core Group meeting ever.

"No, what I mean is, who are we?" Gil repeated, with a rare philosophical glint in his eyes—perhaps even his nostrils were flared a bit philosophically too.

"Successful business executives?" Susan chanced, parting her squinted eyes to make the point and get on with it. She sat up in her chair, hoping to enhance the effect.

Bob caught on. "I'm Big 'N Hard; he's Big 'N Hard," pointing to Matthew, "she's Big 'N Hard, so's he, and Mr. Bateson, you are…BIG 'N HARD!" he announced, shaking the mahogany.

"Yes, we are. That's us. We're all big and hard. So, how's everybody doing? Susan, how are you doing?" Gil inquired, contentedly.

"I'm fine, Gil."

"That's nice. Real nice. Now, what say we start with Bob to get the ball rolling. Bob, what's going on with the financial situation?"

"Uh," Bob began, with a sniff—he seldom used the sniff, took finesse to use the sniff. "We've been throwing a lot of cash at the payroll, Gil. I'd like to be serving more to R and D, for obvious reasons. Hell, I'll state it anyway—we are a growth company. We grow by innovation, aggressive marketing, and consumption of the competition. We take over. We command. Those who do our bidding—those whom we call employees—are lucky to be with us. We haven't dumped them—unless, of course, the economy continues to grow; in that case, we'll have to throw them some more bones." He took a short breather; this was the most meeting effort he'd ever put out. He was actually starting to sweat on his face—not good business. "Anyway, we need to invest in more R and D and in more acquisitions."

"Not doing enough in these areas, are we?" Bateson calmly asked.

"No, we are not. As I am sure Reginald and Matthew will tell you."

Gil glanced over at each of them thoughtfully. They eyed each other unhappily.

"What we need," Bob continued, "is more cash. And sales isn't helping, Susan'll tell you that."

Bateson gazed her way with what she considered to be a dumbass smile.

"I hate to mention the D word," Pridgeon warned.

"You mean debt?" Gil asked, with a sudden expression of shock and horror.

"I didn't want to bring it up."

"The D word?" Bateson said.

"Fuh, fuh, fuh," Matthew attempted to inject. "Fuh, fuh, fuh."

"No, we don't need the F word right now, Matthew, don't get your bra in a bind." Then he stopped himself. "Sorry, Matthew, didn't mean to put it that way. What I mean to say is, keep a cool head, we're not going to take on any debt. Not now, not ever."

Matthew was shaking his head "No," not because of debt per se, but because he'd wanted to discuss his fantastic news. He wanted to launch this with "Fortunately"—an unfortunate first choice.

"Okay, so forget about taking on any D," Bob went on, "Stock price has fallen—what, say, ten, twelve percent—but we could issue some new shares or convertible warrants or even a bond."

"Okay, Bob, sounds good. Write this up for me, will you? Send me a proposal."

"I already did," he responded, edging on exasperation.

"Yeah, right, now I remember. Well, I'll get on it right away, Bob," said Gil, almost nonchalantly. Susan—who usually occupied her time here staring at her coffee mug or the opposite wall—had begun to measure each member's visage in disbelief at what she was hearing. A first indication of fear, not good business.

"Susan," Bateson announced, bringing her back to the front, "what's news from sales?"

"Not bad, but not good. Steady, sales are steady," she replied, trying to steady the nerves, as well. "They will go down though and no amount, or change, in advertising, or any other strategy, will bring them back. We need some new product. Growth in sales rate—of which there is none—has markedly declined compared to accounts receivable and inventory growth rates. Bad news, gentlemen."

"Bad news, huh?" said Gil.

"Extremely bad!"

"Well, we'll have to do something about that then, won't we. This is all you've got to say, Susan?"

She sighed. "That sums it up, Gil." Susan looked him in the eyes—trying to pierce those unusually, but incredibly dull pupils to glimpse the cause, the reason, the short-circuit, the crash in Bateson's operating system. It was then that she realized how distraught she really was—electronic metaphors, for God's sake!

"May I go next, Gil?" Reginald requested, eager to offer.

"Why, yes, Reginald, that would be delightful," he responded in a soothing tone—took all the starch out of Reg, he didn't know if the boss was being sarcastic or just merely totally insane.

"Good then," he hesitated. "Okay, well, it's a video card."

"A video card. Are we doing any video cards right now?" the CEO asked.

"No, but we can and it would be big! The best 3D chip available—gaming industry would eat it up!"

"Big, huh?"

"Big. Fast. A huge RAMDAC of 500, 600 megapixels per second fill rate; uses DDRAM—the fastest; 32 megs onboard…"

"Whoa, whoa, whoa! Need to know here, Reg…I mean, Reginald. So, I take it, it's good, huh?"

"Very, very good," beamed Reginald, exhausted and glowing like he'd recently given birth or had the big O. Needless to say, he appeared spent.

"Very good then, Reg, and I do have a copy of your proposal," Gil stated, with subtle hesitation. Reginald's sails sagged again.

"Yes, sir, I sent it to you last week."

"Yes, I know…and it was real good. Really very good. Okay, so now that we've had some good news, Matthew can you add to this?"

Bateson had never asked for his input in such a calm, easy manner—this was unprecedented at BNH. Didn't help.

"Va, va, va," he said. "Va, va, va," and the others' minds went awandering, each on its own path to what Matthew was actually planning to say. Susan's concluded that it went something like, "Vat do you expect, miracles?" in a Yiddish accent. Bob's told him, "Va, va, va voom!" Reg's went simply, "Va, va, va," as it was supposed to. And Gil wondered if he could get some help for this outstanding executive.

"Video," emerged, unblemished, and hung in the air.

"Va, video cards. Two chipset integrators, solid companies," and with that, Matthew rested, maintained, concentrated. "Choice companies. Should be easy pickings, provided we've got the cash. Got to move on this though—tough market."

"Got to move on it, have we?" Gil asked.

"Ga, ga, ga, got to!"

"Okay then, talk to Bob. We'll see what we can do," Bateson replied, assuringly. "So, gentlemen…and lady," he gazed over at Susan—really bad posture, she should get that checked. "I guess that about sums it up. Lookin' good." He rose from his chair, and nodded, "Lookin' good." The others searched the room for what Gil found so attractive, since the news had not been. Ugly news. Ugly room. Ugly day.

*

Dark paneled midday dining with Susan at The Place was forever something different for Bateson. But they'd been here before. Had a sameness, this Bistro. Early twenties of brown, straight hair re-emerged with much fabled reluctance.

"Good afternoon," she said. "My name is Stephanie. Today's specials are…" here she halted, expecting the worst, remembering the face. But nothing. No verbal slap, no premature review of a lack of acceptable service. She forgot what the specials were.

"Good afternoon, Miss," Gil said politely. "We can see your specials on the chalkboard over there. Please give us a few moments to decide. In the meantime, could you please bring us…" he turned to Susan and asked, "Bottle of Chardonnay?" She nodded. "Stephanie, could you please bring us a bottle of your finest Chardonnay?"

"Yes, sir. Right away," Stephanie replied, with far too much gratitude. "Thank you, sir," and she was off. There was a step to her bounce.

Susan shattered the moment. Not being accustomed to any politeness, proper manners, propriety, any damn decent public relations from the boss—she was thrown off edge.

"Is there something wrong, Gil? Have you got some sort of deadly, incurable disease? Are you dying, Gil? Be honest, is everything okay?"

"Everything is fine, Susan, why do you ask?" he inquired, calmly and sincerely.

"You are acting so fuckin' weird! You are out in left field, my friend. If you don't mind my saying."

"No, Susan, that's fine. I value your opinion."

All this goddamned calmness was going to make her puke, she thought!

"What's wrong, Gil?" she demanded, sharing with a radius of three tables in all directions.

"Not a thing, dear, honestly."

"Dear? DEAR! You have never called me 'dear'! Do you see what I mean, you're acting—if you don't mind my saying—GODDAMN FUCKING WEIRD! What the fuck's up?"

"Now calm down, Susan, would you please? I'm sorry if you find my behavior disturbing. I can't help myself. I simply feel good. Never really felt like this before. Feeling good really feels good," he stated, emphasizing this with a shrug.

"Feeling good really feels good? Where the hell did you come up with that one? Are you watching too much TV, watching all that psycho-shit from fat talk show ladies?" she asked, in blatant distress.

"No, I'm actually devoting a larger portion of my free time to reading. My wife and I have also been taking long walks along the lake more often."

"Your wife?!" she almost screamed.

"Yes, but please, keep it down. Yes, my wife. I've discovered that she's really a rather wonderful person."

"Something is wrong with you, Gil. What, I've known you for ten years? I know you pretty well, Gil, and this is definitely not you. You have never acted like this. You are sick or something. If you know, tell me, what is it?" Stephanie brought and poured their wine. Gil thanked her. Susan downed her glass, grabbed the bottle, and began work on her own solution.

*

"No telling what the man will do next. I can't predict his actions anymore; used to be able to, but not now," Bob told Reginald and Matthew, as they sat at the Bayview on Queen Anne Hill. The top BNH crowd often went here for lunch; it afforded a respectable view down on Elliott Bay, down on downtown.

"He, he hasn't done a thing about the two chipset integrators that I think we should acquire," Matthew stated, having already stretched his vocal cords enough to avoid much of a stumble.

"And as I already informed you, nothing about the new video card, as well. What is wrong with the man, Bob? You know him better than we," said Reginald, as they drank coffee next to an immense window—view of the port in the background.

"He hasn't told me a thing; can't get anything out of the bastard. I get the impression that it might be a personal matter. I don't think he's seeing his girlfriend, what's her name, anymore. Anyway, Reg, may be the girlfriend."

"Well, that seems unlikely. My impression is that Mr. Bateson would not be the kind of man to let some female interfere with profit," Reginald stated, with deep concern—mostly for the profit.

"Yep," offered Matthew, maintaining a high note.

"Gentlemen, we're not going to fix it here. This speculation is, for the most part, a waste of time, I think," Bob said, taking the helm. "The question remains, what are we going to do about it?"

"He, he owns most of the company," advised Matthew.

"He'll have control no matter what we do," Reginald said.

"Yes, we know this. Okay, so assuming the company is going south—reasonable assumption, stock price and projected earnings in the toilet. We can do one of two things. Either convince him to make the right decisions or have one of those, what are they called… interventions. You know, we all sit around him and tell him nicely how much he's really fucking up. Or, we can sell out before the stock price falls in the sewer and find other jobs," Bob stated, raising his eyebrows and folding his arms, to drive home the point.

"Another job?" protested Reginald.

"We, we, we," Matthew began, shaken. "We, we, we." Bob was not in the mood for this, he felt like pointing to the washroom. "We would have to work then."

"Yes, we would never be able to step into positions like we've got. Let's face it, gentlemen, what we've got at BNH is a very sweet deal!" Reginald insisted.

"One helluva sweet fuckin' deal!" Bob agreed.

"Yeah!" Matthew added.

"Let's give it a little time, I think. I guess it's agreed that we don't want to jump ship, for the moment at least," concluded Bob, catching each in the eye to assess his reaction. They all knew that this discussion was a fraud, even if it was good business. Each man for himself was the true business credo. They would not act as a team; this was merely a ritualized drama played out to comfort the players by making things much more confusing.

"What are we?" Bob, asked, inspired by something, but he wasn't sure what.

"In the dumper!" said Reg.

"Yep!"

*

Things were still clean. The house was clean; she made sure that the maids kept it. Estate was well-groomed. And the marriage, spotless slate there too, from what she could tell. But things were not in proper order. Beverly Bateson could not relax into the new ritual that had been adopted—something was up, let down the guard and lose it all. She refused to be sanguine about Gil—too devious!

Inspection complete, front door alingering commenced, Mrs. Bateson was prepared for his return. Mirror check and re-check, for security.

Gong. The door opened, but no Gil entered. Bev peered around the corner to see him gazing at something on the grounds.

"What is it, honey?"

"In that tree over there," he said, pointing to a cedar beyond the driveway loop.

"What about the tree, dear?"

"I think that bird's called a Steller's Jay," he replied, staring at the tree.

"How can you tell?" she said; why do you care, she thought. What kind of game was this? Is he supposed to be totally insane now? How does this play into whatever scheme he's hatched?

"Oh, I saw it coming down the drive. They have a pointed head," said Gil, as he turned and flashed Beverly a smile.

You've got a pointy head—two points…two horns, she imagined. This had been going on for at least a few weeks; hard for her to tell what kind of intricate plot was being woven. And now this bit with the birds. Some goddamn thing was cooking and she was getting worried—bastard was clever!

"How was your day, dear?" he inquired.

Another preemptory strike, she noted. "Fine, dear, how was yours?"

"Outstanding, Beverly, outstanding!" he replied, as his coat and briefcase were removed. "Thanks, sweety," Gil said to the maid.

"You're welcome, sir," she said, as he nodded kindly.

He next grasped his wife by the shoulders, holding her at arm's length, smiling. "Damn, you look good!" Gil admired, inspecting her up and down—pausing at her more intimate regions.

"Why, thank you, Gil, that's so sweet," Beverly responded, managing a slight, but unconvincing smile. When would it end, she wondered. Was there some plan here or has the bastard just gone absolutely nuts? Is he going to want sex again tonight? What the hell did I do to deserve this shit?

"I am ravenous, Beverly. Let's have dinner," he suggested, with enthusiasm and one huge lip plant on her—full contact tongue probe. She hadn't yet grown accustomed to these either; her lips had been so long dormant, tongue wasn't quite in wrestling form. This action literally left her speechless, and stunned. Speechless because Bev couldn't move her tongue. Stunned from worry about this organ—they weren't supposed to go completely limp on you. So there she stood, absolutely helpless, as she forced a rebirth of motion in her flaccid oral appendage.

"I'll be down in a second," Gil announced happily. "Just go up, have a wash," and he ascended.

"Owkayth. Okayth. Okay, dear," she finally blurted, and she sped off to a downstairs bathroom to mop her own face. Everything had been fine, but the bastard had to play his little game.

More really gourmet, fancy shit for dinner, Beverly thought; she couldn't come up with the proper name for it, but she knew it was really very something. They always dined well. She usually talked about the food when they ate together, it was part of the job description—make small talk at the table, food's an adequate topic.

She couldn't muster the neurons necessary to think about this stuff that was being delicately stuffed into their oral cavities. She had to fend off his niceties.

"Beverly, you are absolutely beautiful this evening," Gil said, with sincere adoration.

"Thank you, honey, that's so sweet," she said, coyly, thinking, "What is it, you fucker? Lay it on the table!"

"We need to spend some more time together. I think I'm spending too much time on work, not enough play. I think I'll take a week or two off; we'll take a short vacation. It's almost the end of February, rains a lot this time of year, we'll go someplace dry and warm. What do you say, Bev honey?"

She gazed up at the chandelier, took a deep breath. Together, she thought, there's no way in hell!

"Let me think about it, darling," she said, "I've got clubs and meetings—you know, girl stuff to consider. Can I get back to you on this, honey?" she asked, overloading the sugar. Bastard would probably throw me off some goddamned boat, bury me in some sand dune, feed me to a fucking camel, or some shitty thing, Bev imagined.

"Sure, fine, dear, whatever you'd like," replied Gil with a hint of disappointment.

She was going to burst. Beverly could feel her organs rising, all her hairs too—pushing their way up, further and further. Organ logjam in her throat, shaved hairs resprouting, face like borscht! And the pulse, throbbing in her temples—pounding!

"You know, maybe we could start a little gardening thing in the back somewhere; grow a few vegetables—do a little project together, what do you think?" he asked, with innocent eyes.

"WHAT IS IT?" she shouted, in a surprisingly deep voice. "WHAT'S GOING ON? WHAT DID I DO?" It was amazing how humongous crow's feet could get all of a sudden.

Gil was genuinely taken aback—his turn to be speechless. Shock turned to concern in his countenance and his words followed suit, "Calm down, dear, what's the matter?" he quietly asked, and reached for her hand. She pulled it back, intent on some answer.

"WOULD YOU QUIT THE SHIT? Okay, you win, you've got me, what is it?" she asked, somewhat vented, regaining control. A cook and a maid were still hopeful though, a couple of corners and doors away.

This he had never seen before. This was not the Beverly that he had married, however many years ago, thought Bateson. This would not do. That phrase, the "not do" one, stopped all monologue activity, because this phrase had never been registered in his own personal inventory of clichés. So, now was he not only upset, extremely upset with his wife, he was also put off to some degree with himself. Certainly not beneficial to the digestive processes.

"All right now, what the hell are you screaming about, Beverly?" he spouted, having squelched his anger considerably.

"Let's be frank, Gil, you've been acting strange for a couple of weeks now," she exclaimed, and then turned up the sarcasm, "Dinner downstairs, 'Oh, you look so great, honey,' flowers, hugs, frenching me at the door—all this shit!"

"Excuse me if I sound stupid here, but aren't these the things a good, loving husband is supposed to do?"

"Not you, Gil, not you. You are not a good husband, you are a husband. And I am a wife, not good, but we are married. You go your way and I go mine. Things work out this way. I do the things I'm supposed to do—making you look good in our social circle, things good for business—and we get along fine. And now this. What is it, Gil? What do you want from me? Haven't I been a proper wife? Haven't I done the right things?"

"You're a perfect wife, Beverly, perfect. And I know in the past that I haven't really shown my appreciation. But now, now I know better, and I want to show you. I want to show you how much I appreciate and love you, Beverly," he said, almost pleading—this bothered him, as well, the pleading.

She picked up her serviette from her lap and threw it on whatever gourmet food they'd been stuffing. With wild, likely-to- crack make-up eyes, she ended the conversation, "Fucking bastard!" And she raged out of the dark paneled dining room. Left the why hanging.

Gil stared through the doorspace of her departure for ten to fifteen seconds. Then he decided to finish his meal—it was good stuff.

Chapter 15

"I think they stick a wad of cotton or something in their mouths to make them smile more for the camera," stated Les, convinced of his theory. "It stretches the cheek, pulling it away from the teeth."

"Sorry, that's not it," Ashley replied, from across the round table. They sat next to an enormous window with a view down to Elliott Bay. "I should know, I do a lot of public speaking. It's hard candy, so their mouths don't dry out."

"Okay, that sounds reasonable. Why are we talking about this anyway?" he asked, then remembered he'd brought it up, the TV talk—Subject: what's the lump in a TV newscaster's cheek pouch? Conversations with Ashley were easier when Tracy was around. Tracy was back in the Bay Area, Ben in Ventura, and Steve at home. Ashley's lawyering had brought her up to Seattle for a meeting. Ashley's phone call had brought Les down I-5 for dinner. At the Bayview on Queen Anne Hill—he'd found it on the web—seemed just right.

For what, he wondered, what would happen tonight? There was hope. Hope was lingering, very nonchalant in the shadows. "How have you been doing?" he asked, taking on her eyes with his.

"Okay, I guess. Not the best. I am tired of being a lawyer. One, it's extremely boring, what I do anyway. And two, it can be very nasty."

"Nasty?"

"Like you'd imagine corporate law to be. Corporate dealings, corporate hassles, corporate buggers," she replied, gazing out over the bay.

"Pays the rent, can't be all that bad."

"It is. What about you? What's teaching seventh and eighth graders like? Rewarding?"

"Sometimes, I guess. I hadn't really planned…to be a schoolteacher. The way things ended up," he said, focusing on the tip of the Space Needle.

"You never really told us about what happened to you while you were at Dyce U. out in the Mojave. You were doing research, weren't you?"

"Yeah, it's a long story. Let's not get into it now, I'll tell you about it sometime." Now he was desperate for a topic change, had to make the evening turn on an upbeat. His past was pulling him down, he was reaching. He grabbed his wine glass and took another drink. "This is good wine." Now I'll thrill her with insightful conversation such as this, he thought sadly.

"Well, it's not bad."

"I'm no wine expert. I only said it…"

"That's okay, Les," Ashley said, with softening eyes. "I know."

She knew, he heard. Phew! He had no clue, but if she could know things. If she was aware of what was going on, then all would be fine. Big relief. He smiled at his place setting.

"I'm glad you were able to drive down to meet me," she said, steering the conversation.

"I'm glad you called. I'm always available on weekends—most nights for that matter." That's right, asshole, tell her what a loser you really are, his mind reminded him.

They were at a critical juncture, or so he perceived. She had the reins, all he could do was to be lead wherever she wanted to go. No backseat driving—fatal error. Or so his current theory instructed him. Ideally, she would take him to where he wanted to go, where they both wanted to go. He hoped she was aware of this—he needed to give her a hint. Les reached across the table and wrapped his hands around her left. She grasped the hands with her right and brought them to her chest, up high.

"Oh, Les, it's so good to see you," she murmured sweetly, wide smile. Then she let go.

Either she'd taken the hint and dished it back, or the hint had been too subtle, he surmised. Perhaps if he tried leering—catching her eyes and imagining crazy, yet wholesome sex. Nothing perverted. Not that he ever…just some normal, intense, thoughts of sex. Les assumed The Look.

"I have no social life in L.A. Seems like I'm always working and spending the rest of the time recovering from it," admitted Ashley.

"Like I said, I don't get out much myself." Now we're even, she squared that off nicely, he concluded. Neither was having sex. A jump there, but a reasonable assumption. The Look was working.

"Remember the beach?" she asked, eyes downcast.

"How could I forget?"

"That was nice."

"Yes, very nice." Damn, it's working; okay, keep it cool, he told himself. Steady. She's driving—I'm only along for the ride.

"I guess I couldn't have been more obvious," she said.

"Oh, that wasn't obvious. I was obvious. Anyway, it was very nice." What are we teenagers? Check the speedometer, would you, Ashley? Wasting time here, his mind scolded.

"I guess we sort of feel the same way about each other," said Ashley, still avoiding direct visual contact.

"I think that's a safe assumption." Okay, this is it! Payday! More power to The Look, lower the force field. This latest mental statement, he felt, was somewhat disappointing.

"It's nice that we're taking it real slow," she stated, taking his right hand in hers.

The Look went limp.

*

Both were sitting at one of the tables in the fairly new smoking lounge at BNH. It was cigars only, but even so, most of the personnel preferred the non. There were a couple of other brave chokers shooting pool in the room.

Fred had been joining the others for this daily forty-five minute respite, lately. These days he seemed to be not doing much general managing—demands from above had become less like commandments and more like suggestions. Then there were the rumors.

"Reginald Barrows is getting to be a real pain," Fred said, around the cigar in his mouth. He leaned over the table and quietly continued, "Between you and me…a real asshole! I mean, he always was fairly uptight—nervous, tense, along those lines—but now? Now it's almost impossible to talk to the bastard. He looks like hell too. It's the stress; I think the company's going down the tubes." Both had to lean back at this time, their combined smoke having brought tears to their eyes. That and the intense squinting made them appear entirely nauseated.

"So, you think he'll quit?" asked Steve, at a volume sufficient for the table, but out of reach for the poolers.

"Not only him. You know that woman, head of sales and marketing? The one that resembles that newswoman, Diane Sailor. Always seems hungover. These days, way too hung."

"You think she'll quit too?"

"Or die. Unless she's going through the change of life or something, I don't know."

"What you are saying is that senior management appears to be very upset with the way the company's going?"

"Where have you been? Of course! What I'm saying now is that it's coming to a head. Something's going to bust at the top," said Fred, with a well-worn frown.

"So, we lose one or two senior VP's, they're replaceable aren't they?" Steve asked, calmly blowing his smoke straight up.

"I think it's bigger than that. I think the company's really going under. I'm getting worried."

"Well, I guess I am too then," he replied, straightening up in his seat.

"I'd send out some feelers, check the job market. I mean it."

"Dammit, Fred!" Steve said, way beyond pool range. "I just moved into a new house!"

"That's business these days, my friend. That's business."

*

In the family room of their newly constructed house on the recently developed cul-de-sac, Steve and Rebecca were talking by the sliding glass door. They could watch the kids playing on a red and yellow, molded-plastic climb and slide toy that sat on the fifteen by thirty foot lawn, surrounded by a short chain-link fence—young plants growing along the perimeter.

"Well, Steve, I told you so. We were doing so well. You had a fine job, excellent pay. We bought a new house. The American dream here, Steve. Low crime rate, decent schools. But you had a little pressure at work," Rebecca was saying, rather worked up herself. "A little too much pressure, so you and your ever-so-clever friends decide to play around a little—why not do a little experiment?"

Steve was listening, shifting his gaze from the brown carpet to the kids. He couldn't argue, he had it coming.

"Aw, honey, I'm sorry," she said, realizing that they'd reached the bottom floor. She walked forward the two paces and hugged him.

"I'm sorry, Becky," he whispered into her hair with closed eyes. "I was so damn frustrated. It seemed so damn unreal."

"I know, honey. That's how things are these days, I guess."

"Yeah, but they shouldn't be," he said, still holding.

"Well, they are. And see what happened when you tried to do something about it."

"Yeah, I'm sorry."

"It's okay, honey. Things'll be all right. Things will work out," she replied, patting his back lightly and parting.

The kids were in a sliding frenzy. Climbing the steps, reaching the top, sliding down, running to the steps…

*

The power was there. Sitting right next to him, smiling. All he had to do was to reach over and…he'd had it for a while there, he thought. It got away. Crawling home at belly pace in a Wednesday evening commute. Like yesterday, day before. He had to seize it! *Carpe diem*!

Ben went about his usual routine getting home because on this day it was part of the plan. Pulled into his parking slot, out to check the mailbox. Unlocked the front door, with purpose, and set to it.

No more waiting. She'd called *him* after all those months. Getting together with the others had merely been a way for her to see him. And wasn't the Greed Stopper impressive. He was impressive. He wasn't that damn ugly either—not tall, but not short. He was in the ballpark. He was a player. Should be easy pickin's for a professional like me, he mused. Confidence was pulsing blood to his fingers—and he needed confident fingers. Fingers that could punch the numbers without a second thought. Clear throat too. Everything! Had to be prepared! Stop thinking about it. Get a grip. This stuff is done every day—check out the population figures for certain parts of the world—it can't be that difficult. And most of them don't even have phones. Get on with it. Ben dialed her number.

"Hello," she said.

"Hi, Ashley, it's Ben, how are you doing?" he asked, confident and friendly.

"Oh, hi, Ben. I was hoping you weren't a client."

"Well, I'm not." Duh, he thought. Confidence!

"Yes, I know, Ben, that's why I said that I was hoping you weren't a client. I wouldn't say that to a client. If I did, I wouldn't have too many clients. You see?"

"Yes, I see. I was only making a joke…I'm not a client. Ha, ha."

"Very funny, Ben."

"Yeah, sorry. Anyway, so how're you doing?"

"I'm fine, Ben. How are you?"

"Fine. Fantastic," he blurted. "Yes, doing fine. So, it's been a while, hasn't it." Keep leading the pack, stay ahead of this one, he insisted to himself.

"Yeah, I guess so. A month about, I guess."

"Yeah, that sounds right, about a month." This'll work, he thought, making brilliant observations will really impress her.

"So, what have you been up to, Ben? Making more of that better living through genetics stuff?"

"Better living through genetics—good one," he replied, forcing a forced chuckle. He wasn't sure if she was kidding.

"So how's work?"

"Fine. How's yours?"

"Fine."

Now they'd hit it. That frightening pause—niceties done, time for the entrée—what's the dish? This was a crucial transition. The move had to be made methodically. His call.

"So, anyway, since it's been a month, I was wondering if we could get together some night soon. Dinner, maybe?"

"Well, Ben, I've been very busy lately…"

"Time for a break then."

"I wish I could, but it doesn't seem possible right now."

"Too busy for a dinner?"

"I'm bringing home work every night, Ben."

"Oh, I see."

"Listen, the whole gang is supposed to meet up in Seattle in a couple of weeks, right?"

"Yeah, I think that's what we said."

"The Greed Stopper is supposed to have worn off, or be wearing off at least, right?"

"Yes, it should be effective for two to three months. Mid-December to mid-March, should be right."

"Well, good, so I'll see you then."

"Yes, well…"

"Nice of you to call, Ben, bye, bye."

"Bye, bye," he replied, wishing he hadn't used two "byes." One "bye" was enough. He had completely lost control of that whole conversation, he fretted. She hadn't even been backseat-driving—she'd grabbed the wheel and out-muscled him! Damn she's aggressive! Then Ben had another thought—one of those lightbulb notions. A bright, but insidious flicker.

Chapter 16

Despite all that brave, deceptive talk—that they would act as a unified front to save the company, and their jobs…when Bob, Reginald, and Matthew each separately knew that he'd jump at any time, without any regard to the others' welfare—they ended up doing it anyway. It was a cold business world out there, they couldn't bear the thought of leaving the warm cushions upon which their fat corporate butts were perched. Talk was one hell of a lot of a more reasonable price to pay.

It was the first of March, not yet the Ides, but in keeping with the spirit of clichés—also good business—time for acting the lion. Time to claw for what they had, face the man who would bring them to their knees. They liked the odds, three against one; four, if you included Susan—they hadn't yet spoken this morning. But three of the most powerful men BNH had to offer had called the meeting. It was time. They had left Susan a message with her secretary; hoped she'd be able to make it. It was time to strike!

The three senior VP's assembled in the boardroom about fifteen minutes before the meeting was scheduled. A solid run through before they confronted the CEO—tidy things up ahead of time.

"Okay, so you're going to be the good cop?" Reginald asked Bob. Reginald was quite neatly dressed, but his face was bagged—furrowed brow and eye trenches.

"No, Reg, I told you, there are no cops. Look, if you have to have cops…if you want to play cops, then we're all bad cops. Bad cops, no good cops! Got it?" Bob demanded.

"Yes, all right, we are all bad, got it."

Matthew was keeping silent, but he was very worked up. He was nodding, with one really determined expression—like some street tough, he imagined. Street savvy. Cool under pressure, but ready to explode—make his move.

"You all set, Matt?" Bob asked, excitedly.

Matthew nodded. He kept nodding.

"Got everything you want to say, together?" continued Bob.

Matthew glared at him, nodding.

"We need to make this as effective as possible. We have got to have impact. Matt, you need to be on your best form."

This was too much. Not only was Bob pampering him beyond insult, but all the damned nodding was making Matt nauseous.

"Sh, sh, sh," he started. The others were guessing: sure, should, shut, show, shoot…

"Sh, sh, sh," Matthew said, face straining, neck resisting the nod.

"Shit!" finally emerged in a shout. "Give me a fuckin' break, dammit!"

"Okay, sorry," said Bob, with hushed utterance.

"We are ready now, Bob, you can quit the pep talk. We are as ready as we are going to be," stated Reginald with faltering syllables.

Bateson entered the room as calmly as he had at the previous Core Group meeting. He seemed like that same guy, wearing that same Hawaiian shirt. The hat too—he had that island air about him.

"What's the big emergency, gentlemen?" Bateson addressed the three, as he sat at the table's head.

"We are at a critical point here, a critical juncture," declared Bob, senior VP and point guard.

"Critical, huh," replied Gil. "Say, where's Susan? Hasn't she got to be here to make it official?"

"This isn't a Core Group meeting; this is just a meeting we felt was imperative," said Reginald, hands folded, but tense, on the table before him.

"Imperative, oh, I see," said Bateson, raising his eyebrows, grasping his chair arms. "So, Susan doesn't have to be here?"

"She'll be along as soon as she gets here, I'm sure," Bob said. "But that's not important. Well, it's important, but we can speak for her in her absence. Don't you think?" he said, glancing at the other two for approval. They nodded. Matthew made this a short one, opting for a less nauseating stare at the CEO.

"All right then, Bob, gentlemen, what have you got on your minds?"

"Well, we're worried, Gil…about the company and you. Can't separate the two, really. What's going on?" Bob pleaded. "For over a month now, we have not initiated anything new. Not we, you. None of the materials that we've submitted to you have been acted upon. I will let each man speak for his own department, but I can say generally, Gil, we have had it. This is it!"

"So, this is some sort of ultimatum, is it?" Gil asked, showing little emotion—perhaps a calm hint of a smile.

"I guess that's the appropriate word for it," replied Bob, as he nodded and turned to the others for a similar response—their heads were in sync.

"Okay, so let's have it. What are your demands?"

"The short of it, Gil, is what we suggested at the last Core Group."

"Refresh my memory, would you?"

"You must have all the stuff on your desk or in your computer."

"Yes, I probably do, but since we've gone to all the trouble…" Bateson was saying, as the door opened and Susan's tired mug appeared, followed by a wobbly body. She slumped into a seat, placed the coffee down.

"Have I missed anything?" she asked Reginald quietly, though a private conversation was not possible there—no cubicles.

"No, we're just getting started," he whispered and then realized—bad cops don't whisper.

"Good morning, Susan," said Gil, cheerfully.

"Good morning, Gil," she responded, taking a stab at being bright herself.

"Where were we? Bob, you were going to state your demands."

"I wouldn't really call them demands," Bob suggested, resolve starting to crack.

"Yes, they are," insisted Reginald.

"Yep," said Matthew, eloquently.

"Is this an ultimatum?" asked Susan, showing little concern.

"Yes, it is," answered Reginald.

"Well 'demands' is a word often used with 'ultimatum,'" she advised.

"Okay, okay, but what we don't need is a lot of rhetoric," said Bob.

"But we do have a long established tradition of being open and straight forward at Big 'N Hard," asserted Bateson. "The word 'demand' is the best word for it."

"Yes, Jesus, yes, here are my demands," gasped Bob, loosening his tie and rubbing his eyes. He took a moment to remember what his particular demands had been. "Okay, first, I want to invest in more R and D. To do this and to make acquisitions, we need some cash, So, to sum it up—Gil, I want you to get us some cash and to direct that cash to these areas."

"Okay," said Bateson, without a flinch. "Next."

"I'll go," offered Susan, not knowing that there had been a plan.

"But I..." said Reginald, and stopped himself. All heads turned to him; they watched his countenance turn from pale creases to red folds. "Go ahead," he spurted.

"Well, guys, same story as last time, give me something to work with. We're running out of options here—I need some new product," she said frankly, taking in each members reaction during the silence that ensued. The phrase "running out of options" sounded desperate, didn't sound like BNH—had never been uttered within the Hard walls before.

"Okay, who's next," said Gil, as if addressing an assembly-line.

"That would be me," stated Reginald, wondering if this intervention was actually working. Didn't seem to be, but he was no expert. He felt like hell; he was realizing what a considerable portion of his life was tied up in Big 'N hard.

"I WANT TO MAKE THAT GODDAMNED VIDEO CARD!" he screamed, and stood there, staring at the opposite mahogany surface.

"Is that all?" asked Bateson, unfazed, seated, still holding the chair arms.

"That's all," he managed, missing something.

"Okay, that leaves you, Matthew," Gil said, turning to the final member.

This had not gone at all as he had expected. At this point, Matthew had imagined himself and the others to be standing over a desperately lost and bewildered CEO, under a bright light, as they made demands—one after another after another—as he acquiesced and acquiesced. Matthew, himself, would be nodding at this point.

"Um," he said, without a stutter, impressed by this feat. "As I said before, and it still applies—amazingly—we should acquire those two chipset integrators. With those firms under our belt and the new video card, we should be sitting pretty."

They sat in awe.

Bateson shook it off, and said, "Is that it? All right then, I'll assume there's a time frame for this?"

"Two weeks," answered Bob.

"Right, two weeks. And if by this deadline I don't act upon your demands, I assume you will all be tendering your resignations. Am I correct?"

"Yes," "Yeah," "Yep," were returned.

"So, I'd better get busy then," Gil said, standing up, straightening his jacket. "See you later," he concluded, leaving the room and the others standing around the table.

*

It might have been where pioneers of old used to congregate. Doubtful. Old habits—the team was re-assembling at the Homesteader's Inn, Pioneer Square. The Square. Waiting for Steve.

One table, two conversations—one all female, the other male. Conversations often involved sex or were arranged around it. Current Sex Conversation theory held that it was more comfortable this way.

"A Kingdome today, a dome thought tomorrow," said Tracy, on one of her TV jags. She'd just seen some local news—the five o'clock and five-thirty shows—harping on the fact that the Seattle Kingdome was to be imploded in about two weeks. Top story, great fodder.

"Really annoying, isn't it Tracy. Especially the second or third time around," said Ashley, hoping for sports and weather.

"It's only a damn building," Tracy complained, though she was easing down from where she began—entirely and absolutely incensed.

"There are many 'small town' phenomena that seem to go on in Seattle. The dome is a big part of the cityscape, they're going to miss it."

"They're getting a new sports arena—huge tax drain."

"So, if they're willing to pay for it…" said Ashley, shrugging.

On the other side of the table.

"Women going after very much older men," said Ben, clarifying his position.

"Makes sense, evolutionarily speaking; they go for the established males—increases their chances for successful reproduction," Les replied.

"Then why does society look down upon it?"

"Society's not always up on current evolutionary theory."

"They rag, 'She's going after a father figure,' isn't that a shame?" said Ben, in mock whiney.

"Father figuring."

"Daddy-diving."

"As in dumpster?" asked Les. Ben smiled and rose to get another pitcher of Mai Tai. He was wearing a flower in his lapel.

Steve arrived, as Ben was returning with the rejuvenated jug. The big man had seen better days, much happier ones, no doubt. This was not a mere end-o-the-workday slump—this slump had a load of slump on the side. Steve had no intention of messing with Mai Tai, so Les got up to get him a beer.

"What's with the flower?" asked Steve, head sagging.

"Oh, the boutonniere? Thought I'd try it out. Something different," answered Ben, with a guilty grin, that the others likely took to be slight embarrassment.

"Oh, just trying it out," Steve responded. "What have you got under those slacks? Just trying out some nylons, perchance?"

"The sexy, netted kind with a garter belt," said Ben, flickering his eyebrows.

"Oooh la la," admired Steve.

"What's 'oooh la la'?" asked Les, as he returned and placed the mug before him.

"Thanks," said Steve.

"Ben and Steve are talking about cross-dressing," Tracy offered, as she leaned her elbow on the table, chin on the hand.

"And it's fascinating," noted Ashley, adopting Tracy's enthused body language.

"I see and this is all I missed?" asked Les, as he took chair.

"Okay, folks," said Ashley, "let's get on track here—ladies' fashions later. So, why don't we fill up our glasses and let Steve do the talking." They all silently agreed. Ben filled all the glasses, following the instructions of this beautiful, yet way too assertive, female. Les was glad to get on with it; he liked her style. Tracy wasn't much interested in discussing ladies' fashions.

"We could have done this over the phone," Steve suggested, and let out a sigh.

"We felt that we actually had to see you, Steve, to get a clear picture of what has been going on. You can't get a clear picture over the phone," replied Ashley, sitting now erect in her seat.

"I told you most of it over the phone."

But, that was a week ago," stated Tracy, mimicking Ashley's attentive posture.

"And it's been a lot of the same."

"Come on then, Steve, let's have it. Lay it out," insisted Ashley. Conversation was on autopilot, so Ben and Les were sitting back for the ride.

'Let's see, oh yes, they aren't mere rumors anymore. Rumors have been confirmed and re-confirmed—the company is going belly-up. Bateson went off his nut, somewhere around two months ago, and quit doing anything. Except for the perks and promotions and pay raises that he authorized for BNH employees. But we've flat-lined. Any day now, senior personnel are going to quit—when that happens, it's all over."

"So, you're feeling kinda crappy now?" Tracy asked, sounding very "I'm with you."

"You might say that," said Steve, pulling on his beer.

"How do you feel, Steve?" Ashley probed, her intense expression having melted into one of deep concern.

"Pretty low, right now. Having to search for another job. Possibly, or probably having to re-locate—and we just bought the new house."

"Worse than how you felt before we sprayed him?" Tracy inquired.

"One helluva lot worse. Then you were merely worried about losing some benefits or a change of job status. Now, it's so damn unpredictable. Nice perks, but it's kind of like the Titanic."

"No, don't use that one," said Les. He was sympathetic, but not the Titanic.

"The Hindenberg would work," suggested Ben, equally concerned, but the clichés.

"Okay, sorry, the Hindenberg then."

"Come on you guys! Let Steve talk," admonished Tracy.

"Sorry," "All right," followed.

"The Hindenberg is as tired as the Titanic," Ashley observed.

"I'm sorry," Ben almost shouted, but kept it on "replied loudly."

"In any case," Steve continued, pulling them out of their logjam, as they sat near "skid row"—though he wasn't thinking "logjam," trying as he was to avoid trite phrasing. "Things could be worse, perhaps. That's it, plain and simple."

"So, it didn't work," concluded Tracy.

"Yes, it did," replied Ben. "It simply didn't come out like we wanted it to."

"How did we want it to come out?" asked Les, wondering if he'd only forgotten.

"We wanted to see if there was a way by which we could manipulate greed in society. Our perception was that our society was too filled with greed; this was our attempt to stem it," concluded Tracy.

"And it didn't work. Society would go down the dumper," stated Tracy.

"It did work," Ben demanded.

"Well, maybe we could cut the dose in half," suggested Tracy.

"It's not over yet," advised Les, perhaps too quietly. Steve was too tired to throw in any of his sense.

"We wanted to stop greed," said Ben. "We stopped it. We're just not happy with the consequences."

"We don't have consequences yet," Les reiterated. "It's not over," this time with more on the volume crank.

"That's right!" shouted Ashley, but only a four table radius shout. "It…is…not…over. The stuff is wearing off. Who knows what will happen?"

"I hope it's good," opined Steve.

"Sure," said Ashley. "Everything may work out perfectly. BNH'll get back on its feet—back to its highly predatory, uncaring self. And you've got your new perks, Steve. Things may turn out to be fine," offered Ashley, gazing up at the dark ceiling of the Homesteader's Inn saloon.

"Or not," said Les.

Chapter 17

It was a clear day, ideal for holding the meeting off-site. But this was too big. None of this could be aired in public. The potential for a scene was too immense—falling apart before a crowd too awful to contemplate. Gil wanted to have it on his yacht; the others were titanically opposed.

"Before we begin," said Bateson.

"Hold on, Gil, Reginald's not here yet," Bob interjected.

"Yes, I was getting to that. I am sorry to say, folks, but we have lost our friend, Reginald. He committed suicide last night."

"What?" "Oh," "Wow!" followed.

"It appears that he hung himself with mouse cords," Gil said, solemnly.

"Did he leave a note?" asked Susan, white-knuckling her coffee mug.

"No note," answered Bateson. "He was a friend and valued member of the Core Group. We'll miss him. His parents are coming down from Bellingham to make the funeral arrangements; you'll all be notified."

For a moment, all were silent.

"Now, down to business," announced Bateson, raising the tempo and volume. "Well, you gave me two weeks. During the last two weeks, did I do a lot of soul searching? Naw. Did I fret over how the company was going to survive? To be honest, a little. What I did mostly, gentlemen, was to take a look at the big picture." He paused for a moment, creating a picture frame with his hands in the air in front of him. Once this was in focus, he continued. "That picture was not a nice picture. That picture was flawed. What I saw was a picture of a highly successful firm being thrown to the dogs for no reason!" Bob and Susan were starting to sweat. Matthew was beginning a shake. Bateson was still evaluating the air picture before him. "You did your jobs. No flies on you. You warned me, supplied me with appropriate solutions once things started going south—but I sat there, and…did…not…do…one…thing. I have no explanation. Maybe it was some mid-life, delayed mid-life crisis, some hormonal thing. I can't tell you," he declared, sound rising, arms moving from frame to palms up, "I have no idea," position. Then one arm dropped, the other made a fist. "BUT…I CAN TELL YOU THIS…I'M BACK, GENTLEMEN, AND I'M BIG 'N HARD!" Matthew almost fainted; Susan almost puked; Bob almost cried. Gil was frozen, standing at the head of the table, frozen with a fist in front of his face. The others caught their breaths. It felt like a minute, maybe two—he thawed, and calmly sat down.

There was a light rapping at the door, and then it opened. In came a neatly dressed, smartly groomed man, who greeted Gil.

"Good afternoon, Mr. Bateson," he said, holding his briefcase by the handle with both hands.

"Good afternoon, ah…Stuart. Folks, I want you to meet Stuart, ah…" Bateson paused, with a puzzled expression.

"Volkmann," Stuart said.

"Thanks, Stu, Volkmann," explained Gil.

"Sir, that's Volkmann with the V pronounced like an F," corrected Stuart. He didn't feel as if it was the proper time to inform the boss that he preferred to be addressed by his full name, Stuart.

"Fine, Stu, fine. Mr. Ffolkman," Bateson replied, stopping a moment to let his exaggerated F sink in, "will be the new Senior Vice President and General Manager of the Technology and Manufacturing Group. Stu comes from…oh, I forget the name of the company, he'll tell you. Anyway, Stu, here, is Reg's replacement. Highly qualified, etc., etc., and he's had some time—since this morning, I guess—to get up to date on what T and M has been up to. Is that about right, Stu? Here," Gil said, gesturing, "take a seat."

"Yes, sir, that about sums it up," replied Stuart, as he sat.

"Nice to meet you, Stu," piped Bob. "I'm Bob Pridgeon, CFO." They shook across the table.

"Hello, Bob, nice to meet you too. Please call me Stuart, would you? I prefer my full name."

"Sure Stu...art," said Bob, glancing over at Gil with either a "get a load of him" or a "here we go again" expression. This passed right over Susan's coffee mug and Matthew was too occupied preparing for his introduction.

"And this is Susan Glumm, Senior VP Sales and Marketing, and Matt Zonk, Senior VP Corporate Business Development."

"Hi," "Hello," followed, along with handshaking.

Bob was beginning to blush. Bateson's old mannerisms, what he'd said, the feel, this feel to the meeting—it was right. Bob was feeling like he could just burst with joy. Susan was still coming out of her morning fog. Matthew was lamenting Stuart's last name.

"Stu's up on our recent, well, current crisis," Gil said, watching the new employee. "I think we'll find that he is Big 'N Hard material. Now, down to specifics. Stu, like what we discussed, get on with that video card now, full bore. For this we need cash. So, okay, Bob, you need to get together with that guy in Human Resources—what's his name—and do some squeezing. Change some jobs from full to temp, reduce some benefits, that sort of thing." He glanced over at Pridgeon and Bob smiled. "Susan, we'll get to you in a second. Matt, start negotiations. I assume those two are still available and you've done all the tirekicking?"

"Yep."

"Very well, then, these'll have to be LBO's. I know," Gil continued, gazing around the room at faces and walls, the paintings, "you thought you'd never hear the D word at BNH. Well, I'm saying it. Bob, you know what to do. We're taking on some big D, but short term; we'll dump it soon enough."

"Right on it, chief," promised Bob, immediately regretting the brown that he just got on his nose.

"Now, Susan," he said, turning to Sales, "I guess you can figure out what to do given all this." There were times at BNH when precise verbiage was simply not effective communication. Gil could have merely grunted and shaken his head at Susan and she would have got the gist.

"It'll be a pleasure, Gil, pure pleasure," she said, smiling, chin on table, arms outstretched.

"Oh yeah, one more thing though, Sue. Expand our presence on the E…or I. I want more E-marketing. Let's do more E-commerce, okay?"

This rubbed off some of her smile, took a bit off the sides. "Sure, Gil, will do," she exclaimed, sitting up, knowing it was for the best, good business.

"Now," said Bateson, sharply, "we're going to introduce a new concept for BNH. An idea that had played out well for other comp. companies. I want it to work for this comp. company. It will be known only by the initial. The entire word will never be spoken or written. It will only be known as M. We are going after the big M. In what, you ask? Are the fields not all filled?" He let the question hang, pregnant in the breeze. "What concerns Americans these days? Fifty percent divorce rate—if it were up to us, it would be even higher, am I right?" he chuckled, the others chuckled. "Growing gap between rich and poor—and growing—go, go, go! Gun control—Big Bang Theory. And," he stopped here, effective tool, silence, "VIDEO GAMES!" he shouted, arms held out to God or the ceiling.

The room was stunned.

"How are we going to get a big M on video games, Gil? There's way too much competition," stated Bob, a bit disappointed.

"We, my friend, are going to find a way. Do some research. We're already turning in that video direction; we'll simply put a little more crank on that turn."

"Do you think, realistically, that we'll ever be able to destroy enough of the competition to have a big M?" asked Stuart, feeling that he had enough leverage to join in.

"I am not absolutely certain, Stu. Not 100 percent. But we've made miracles happen before at BNH, so I figure, why stop? Why let words like 'impossible,' 'no way,' 'ridiculous,' get in the way?"

"You're the boss, chief," said Susan.

"Let's get it, Gil, let's take on a big M!" declared Bob, caught up in the insanity.

"Muh, muh, muh," uttered the previously silent Matthew. "Muh, muh, muh!" They all knew what he meant. Stuart assumed it was in some code.

"I'm feeling confident about all this. Can I assume we're all on board?" Gil asked.

"Yes," "Yeah," "Right," "Ya, ya," followed.

"Gentlemen, that makes me happy. I can feel it. Can you feel it? Do you know what this makes me? Do you know what this makes us?" he asked, yelling like a goosed Baptist preacher.

"BIG 'N HARD!" three of them responded. Stuart was impressed.

*

She was not sure if the "effect" would ever matter again. Big lump in her throat every evening. Expect the unex...bastard could do anything! Nylons, skirt/blouse or dress, earrings, high heels—Beverly was nine yarding it every night, just in case.

She gave the maid a once over. Everything seemed perfect. Beverly thought herself much prettier than the maid. Beverly thought herself much prettier than all of her girlfriends, the ladies in her social circle. What more could the man want? The toll interrupted her thoughts.

"Hi, honey," she said, as he opened the door. She pecked him and asked, "Have a nice day? See that pointy head bird again?"

"Fine, fine, Bev. Pointy head what?" he asked, blank stare directed her way.

"The bird. The Starry Jailbird or something?"

"Oh, the bird. No, I didn't see it."

"Did you have a nice day, honey?" At least no fuckin' bird talk, she acknowledged.

"Fine, dear, fine," he said, allowing himself to be shed of coat and briefcase. She expected him to make the next move. She waited, anticipating some form of embrace, cringing.

"Well, I expect your day was fine, was it?"

"Yes," she replied to this new twist to the interrogative.

"Well, it usually is, isn't it?"

"Yes," she said, liking the sound of that. Bit on the gruff, uncaring side. Promising.

"Listen, you won't mind if I catch dinner upstairs tonight, will you? I mean, I know our pattern had been to dine together lately, but I really had one hell of a day. It was fine, but it was still hell. I am really beat."

"Oh, I'm sorry dear," she replied, desperately hopeful—difficult to sound sympathetic.

"Yes, well, I think it should be an early for me tonight, Beverly. This may be the way it goes for the next week or two—tough times at BNH."

"Tough times?" she said, thinking—tough big and hard times at last.

"A little re-structuring, not to worry," he replied.

"That's good, dear."

"So, could you have my dinner sent up?" he asked, patted her on the shoulder without waiting for a response and bounded up the staircase.

"Certainly, dear," she said to the maid. "Whatever you like, my beautiful fucking bastard!"

The maid blushed. Beverly waited until she heard a door close upstairs, then she began a sprint to the back of the house, almost tripping over another startled maid. Out a door she went, reached up for the sky, and screamed, "FUCKIN' BASTARD'S BACK!"

Charlie, the elderly gardener who was working on the Boxwood with a manual hedge-trimmer, glanced up and over at the Mrs. She didn't see him. Charlie was a bit hard of hearing, but at least he got the "back" part of the message.

"You want 'em cut back more?" he shouted, scaring the hell out of the Mrs., who had thought that she was addressing the garden alone.

"Shut up!" she snapped.

*

It was all coming back to him. Parking by Alki Point as he had so many times—back to business was the plan.

He knocked on her door; a curtain parted to his left. Noises of movement, hushed voices, confusion slipped under the door. Dolly opened it in a Leopard patterned robe; she still had that puffy hair, some puff to her eyes, as well.

"Gil what a surprise! What brings you here?" she said, from a wide crack in the doorway.

"Dolly...well? Aren't you going to ask me in?" he asked, arms extended in anticipation of their traditional grapple-dance. She let him hang, glanced back into the condo.

"Sure, honey, come on in," she replied, widening the crack.

He entered; an immediate bang and "umphh" emanated from the bathroom. Not normal empty potty sounds anyway, Dolly surmised.

"You got company?" Bateson asked, as he took a seat in the easy chair.

"Yeah, sorta," Dolly admitted, standing a few paces back with her hands hipped. "But you never said I couldn't have company. You said you wanted me to find a good man." Then a mid-twenties, clean-cut, bring-home-to-Mamma man emerged with a shirt that needed better tucking, and said, "See ya, Dolly," almost before you could witness the door slamming.

"Company, huh?"

"Gil, it got lonely. I couldn't help it. You never said I couldn't. Is it okay?" she asked, meekly.

"Did you use protection?" he asked, sounding like a concerned parent—uncomfortable image, he shook it off.

"Yes, of course," Dolly replied, matter of factly, standard procedure.

"Good then, no, it's not okay."

"What? But I used protection!"

"So, you're not going to pass anything along to me."

"Well, how could I, we're not…"

"That's my surprise, Dolly. That's why I'm here. We're back! It's on again!"

"You mean back to the way we were?"

"Yes, honey, yes!"

"Well, thank God for that," she responded, holding back a flood of sarcasm. Disappointment, anger. Not a good day. "So, do you want me to…" she asked, pointing to the bathroom.

"Naw, not today, Dolly," he said, recalling the untucked shirt and her puffiness, "Maybe later in the week."

"Okay, Gil," she sighed. "Whatever you want." Her shoulders couldn't sag any lower. She let her arms hang limp as she walked.

Bateson stood and adjusted his belt, unable still to shake that tucking picture. He walked to the door and took the knob. She followed, expecting to kiss him, but his free hand waved her off, as he said goodbye.

Once he was out of earshot, a strident, "GODDAMMIT!," sang out of Dolly's domain.

Chapter 18

The lights flickered sometimes. You could be micropipetting, loading a gel—something that required the highest degree of concentration—and the damned lights would blink. Cheap bastards! But anything could disturb Ben these days. Any little shitty...the place was so staid, like a morgue. Working at Tailored Genetics was like rubbing elbows with corpses. Ben was holding his gaze on a particular light overhead, counting the flickers.

"Good morning, Ben," blurted Eugene, almost knocking him off his stool.

"Jesus, Gene, could you try not to jolt me every time you come in?" replied Ben, with newfound boldness. Impoliteness, sincerity? He wasn't sure, but he knew that giving the boss a little lip wasn't going to cost him his job. He had some security there. He put out.

"Sorry, Ben," said Eugene, not accustomed to such boldness. Eugene considered himself the section's bold one; he was the head. But besides that, he was the one issuing all the orders. He commanded. "I'll try to enter more quietly if that pleases you," he quipped.

"Well, you don't have to fucking shout!"

"Hey, Ben, we don't use that kind of language here!"

"We just did!"

"What's the deal here, Ben? Are you screwing the President's daughter? Have you suddenly developed lifetime job security?"

"You're going to fire me because I didn't like the way you persistently disturbed my concentration."

"So, what had you been concentrating on there, Ben, the miracle of electricity?" Eugene was standing about ten feet to the right of him with his arms folded tightly to his chest. Ben remained perched on his stool.

"No, on what an asshole you could be."

"So, now you're calling me names. It stops right now, Ben," Eugene barked, taking control. "I am your superior—keep this up and I'll fire your ass."

Ben suddenly realized that he'd gone too far. Reality nudged his nerves. "Sorry, Gene, you don't deserve this. I haven't been myself lately." He stopped; he'd sworn, or thought he had, never to utter that phrase in his life! Yet, he'd uttered!

"What is it, Ben? What's wrong?" his boss asked, gone from indignant and really pissed off, to a concerned old friend. This was another of his fine attributes as a leader, another bullet in his arsenal—his ability to change his emotions on a dime.

"It's a woman," Ben offered, being unusually candid. And he'd only realized the reason himself that moment.

"Women."

"Yeah, women."

"Well, that explains it then."

"It does?"

"Sure, guy like you. Professional, financially set, unmarried…"

"Yeah." Ben hadn't considered how really pathetic he was.

"And these days, with all the STD's out there. Viruses. It's a minefield out there, Ben."

"Well, Gene' it's merely one woman."

"A bomb waiting to explode."

"No, not really. She's not explosive, just tough to figure. I can't…"

"I know what you mean, Ben," comforted Eugene.

"I guess you do," he replied.

"Well, sorry for catching you at a bad time. Keep on with what you're doing. We'll forget about all of this," announced Eugene, and he departed.

"Thanks, Gene," replied Ben, as he watched the boss leave. "Prick," he added.

*

Rebecca was planting annuals in the bed along the fence when Steve arrived home from work. The kids were busy on the climb and slide. April brought less rain, warmer air.

"Hi, kids," "Hi, Daddy," rang out.

"Are those pansies?" Steve asked, closing the sliding glass door. He knew four or five flower names.

"Oh, hi, Steve. No, petunias. Do you want me to plant some pansies, dear?" she inquired, on muddy knees with gloved hands, backside toward him.

"A fine aspect," he remarked.

"What was that, dear?"

"Nothing, Becky, not one thing."

"What?"

"Nice plants. That'll be pretty."

"How was work?"

"I think everything is going to be okay. We're back in business."

"No strange changes today? Have you heard any substantial rumors?" she asked, busy with a trowel; popping plants out of plastic packaging.

"No rumors, only what I've seen posted and what Fred has told me," he replied, swatting his kids playfully as they ran around to the steps.

"So, what's the word?"

"We're back to normal, I'd say, back to the way we were. There's a threat of some layoffs now, that's normal. There might be some medical benefit cutbacks, but that's still being discussed."

"Sounds good...damn, what a twisted..."

"All this means is that the company is back on its feet and the claws are out. It's good. These things won't mean the end of us."

"But the crap we have to put up with just to have a measure of security."

"Is the crap we have to put up with. That's business."

"Anything else?"

"Let's see, oh yeah, we recently swallowed up another couple of small companies; they're being fitted."

"Now they've got you using their jargon."

"Becomes sort of second nature when you keep hearing it over and over."

Rebecca stood and turned around to face her husband. Her expression was inquisitive.

"You're not turning into a blood-thirsty, guilt-free, company man, are you, Steve?"

"No, dear," he said, walking over and lightly embracing her. He whispered into her ear, "I only want us to have what we need, that's all."

"Okay, dear," she said softly in return, not able to hug him herself because of the muddy gloves.

*

Meet her half way. That's the way it was supposed to work, according to current Sex theory. San Francisco was close enough to half way. One hour up from L.A., an hour and a half down from Seattle. He would have gone all the way down, but that was L.A.

The Armada at The Wharf, familiar territory. His plane had been more fleet, he mused, as if there existed a spectrum of jet speeds outside of regular or SST. Wind could be a factor—fair or foul. Les was having a vodka tonic in the Captain's Quarters downstairs, awaiting his ship to come in. They'd gone slow—time for him and Ashley to go fast.

She arrived precisely at one point three vodka tonics, so everything seemed to Les to be going according to plan. And she was beautiful. Not three pitcher, four scotches, or however many…she was plain gorgeous.

"Hi, Les," she said, he rose, they hugged. Then she planted a kiss on him that gave his tongue monumental muscle memory. On approach to fast, he thought.

"I missed you," she confessed, as they sat. Ashley ordered two vodka tonics from a passing waiter.

"I missed you," Les replied, thinking what a clever choice of words.

"This is going to be fun," she said, eyes locked onto his. He pined for the definition of "fun."

"Yes, spring in The City," he said, happier with that one.

Their drinks came; each used one hand for glass, the other for hand holding. Les began to feel something rubbing his leg, but he had been fooled before. This, he assumed, was his own peripheral nervous system playing some sick gag on his central nervous system—at his expense. They drank for a while.

"Let's go upstairs," Ashley suggested, in one blatantly seductive, low whisper.

Only two point three drinks, this was no mirage. He was prone to seeing mirages, Les cautioned himself.

"Have you registered?" he asked, as they stood.

"You've got a room, haven't you?"

Not a mirage, his central nervous system confirmed. Fast, going fast now—SST.

*

1500 boats, mostly sailboats, packed onto twenty-four docks was Shilshole Marina. But it wasn't very crowded on a weekday—usually a great place to hold a quiet meeting on a clear April afternoon. Mid-April, but the accountants were taking care of the taxes; not the Group's burden, as they gazed west upon the white-capped, sharp peaks of the Olympics. Matthew was sitting on deck wondering about words, as he often did. It was the derivation of the name, Shilshole. Didn't sound native. Some guy named Shil used this bay as a refuge? A place where shills congregated? Another one that bothered him was, in fact, where he was sitting. A cockpit. Obvious reasons.

That thought had occurred to Susan, as well. Funny name for the place with the steering wheel. She, herself, had used the term, but in a vastly different context, and in jest, sort of.

Stuart was still getting a feel for the firm. He grasped the rigging and stared up beyond the top of the mainmast. This was where one would find a Crow's Nest, he mused. This was where he was headed—to the top. Stuart was a mover—a sailor, at present—though captain Gil had no intention of untying and taking them out for a sail. Too much like work.

Instead of weighing anchor, Bob was occupied with a decision—to relax and have a cocktail or to relax and have a beer. He decided to relax and let these questions answer themselves. Leaning back, Bob was, when...

"Avast ye swabs!" boomed Bateson. "What are we?"

"BIG 'N HARD!" shouted the three, fists punching the sky. Stuart felt left out.

"Big 'N Hard!" shouted Stuart, better late th...They all stared at him, somewhat put off; he'd fairly spoiled that one.

"Everyone doing okay?" asked Gil. "You got your drinks, something to eat?" None complained. "Okay then, folks, let's get down to business and get it over with. Bob, why don't you do the honors."

"You got it, Gil," beamed Bob. "Okay then, so you'll all be glad to know that we've got some cash and we've already started to put it to some good use. We have taken on some big D, but it's short term—not to worry. We've also done some right-sizing, so I'd say we're back on course."

"Back on it, eh, Bob?" asked Gil.

"Back on it."

"All right then, how 'bout you, Matt, what's the word on those two LBO's?"

"Duh, duh, duh," said Matthew, slightly startled by being the next one called. "Duh, done," with pride he stated. "Working on them as we speak."

Bateson was impressed. Not so much by the successful takeovers, but by the fact that Matt had been able to pass this news on with such efficiency. Was a cure close at hand?

"Outstanding, Matt, outstanding," Gil proclaimed. "We're on a roll here, folks. We're steam rollin', baby!" They all watched a pair of gulls flying overhead, concerned about any crap that might fall their way.

"Stu, what's new?" inquired the boss.

He had already decided to wait another month or so before insisting upon that change of address. Stu was far too familiar for a man of his status, he'd concluded—sounded like a cheap meal.

"The new video card will be ready for production in two weeks," he proudly stated.

"Two weeks? Are you for real, Stu?" asked Gil.

That stung, but he replied, "Yes, sir, Mr. Bateson, two weeks."

"Well, that's excellent news, Stu. But, ah, don't call me Mr. Bateson, we're informal here. Call me Gil."

"Okay, Gil."

"Good, Stu, good. So this new card, Sue, tell me how superior it's going to be. What fantastic things are going to happen at BNH?"

"Focus is on the card, chief! Reg was right and Stu has carried it through. Are you ready for a video game that'll just reach out and grab you by the balls?" she asked with piercing eyes; the rest of the group felt pierced, or at least kneed. "Or whatever you got down there? 3-D images from this monster can literally do it. Boobs and butts jumping out of the screen; explosions so real you can feel them in the pit of your heart—pick an organ. As close to virtual as you can get without all the hook-ups. Gil, you want the big M—this'll give us the goose we need to get it!"

"The big G!" insisted Stuart, boldly. The others glared at him, unenthused.

"We don't call it the big G, Stu," advised Bob, with an understanding tone. "It's a goose; we use the word, goose."

"Sorry."

"That's okay," said Bob.

Stuart decided to proceed with more caution. He had carried the ball with the video card, but he was missing too many of the other calls. "The big M, it's not spelled m-e-r-g…" he asked.

"No," blasted Gil. "More like m-o-n-o…perhaps," he stated, with a wink.

"I got ya," said Stuart, now in on it—an insider.

"Good, Stu, good," replied Bateson, sharing a hint of suspicion with the rest of the Core Group. "Now, where were we?"

"Well," continued Susan, "we've got to come up with one incredible name for it. We're working. Something very destructive sounding like Mindgrinder or something."

"I'm sure you'll come up with a perfect one, Sue," Bateson said. "When it comes to destructive thinking, you're the tops!"

"Thank you, Gil, that means a lot," she gushed.

"And I mean it." Bateson let those words waft for a while, as each recovered from the sentimental lapse that they'd experienced.

"All right, folks," he concluded. "Oh yeah, Bob, you forgot to mention that the share price has rebounded some since we made that little goose," Gil took a moment to make sure that Stuart had heard the word, "with the stock buyback. We're back on the warpath, gentlemen! We will get rid of the big D and make a big M!" Shouting now, he asked, "Who are we?"

"BIG 'N HARD!" responded all four.

Having hit that one, Stuart felt a spurt of pride. He gazed up at where the Crow's Nest would be—gave him yet another inspiration.

"Hey, what about internet sales?" he mentioned.

"Meeting's over, Stu," scolded Matthew, head bobbing.

Chapter 19

Cubicles weren't all that bad, once you thought about it. Saved on door knocking, easy to decorate, and wide open space above the walls. You weren't alone in the world in a room full of cubicles. Steve wondered why he'd been so pessimistic about this fine invention.

"Good morning, Steve," was the bald and short greeting given by Fred Gompers. He was busy squeezing some contraption for improving his wrist strength. Fred didn't usually shake hands when he was making his morning rounds.

"Morning, Fred," said Steve, swiveling and returning from his space thinking. "Working on your grip?"

"I am improving the strength of my wrists—a little exercise program," Fred explained.

"A program?"

"Routine. I don't know what to call it."

"Getting in shape?" asked Steve to the GM's belly.

"It's a start, anyway. A positive step," his boss stated, somewhat irritated at all of this sudden interest in his personal agenda.

"It's good, Fred. A good thing to exercise," noted Steve, holding back a grin.

"Well, I'm not here to talk about how I'm keeping my hands busy. We have some business to discuss, you got a few minutes?"

Sure, Fred, take a seat." He sat on the metal chair at the closer end of the desk. "Bad news?"

"Well, probably not bad for you, but I thought it would be better for me to pass on this information personally, rather than post another impersonal memo—given all that has happened these past few months."

"Sounds serious," said Steve, looking positively sanguine.

"You know about these two new acquisitions that we recently made?"

"The integrator firms?"

"Yes."

"And you're going to tell me that there'll be some more belt-tightening at BNH as they're being assimilated."

"Well, yes. Have I already talked to you about this?"

"No, Fred, this is simply BNH SOP. Now you're going to tell me that I might get laid off, right?"

"Again, yes," replied Fred, wondering if a memo would have been the better option.

"Okay, Fred, message received. I might get laid off," said Steve, showing no emotion.

"Are you feeling all right, Steve? You seem to be taking the news rather well."

"Fred, this is the news I want to hear."

"You like this news? Come on, Steve, you don't need to be sarcastic. Good news—bullshit."

"No, not bullshit, Fred. Let's go over the probabilities here. Let's say I've got a fifty percent chance of getting laid off—if so, chances are I'll get rehired as a temp, for a while. At least I don't have to find another job and relocate."

"Yeah, but you'll make less money, fewer benefits."

"But I'll get them back. At least I won't lose everything all at once."

"I see your point."

"So, it's good."

"Maybe I'll try this approach with the rest of the people."

"If you want, but I'm sure they already know. These things happen. It's the best you can hope for in the business world."

Fred walked to the next cubicle wondering who gave whom the bad news.

*

The Greed Team had decided upon The City for its final convention because this was where it had all begun—should be where it ended.

They'd had a Saturday of bike riding in The Park, buying collectible tourist paraphernalia at The Wharf, and Frisbee on Marina Green—one full day of urban outdoors. All had enjoyed that place on The Pier, knowing full well that it was designed to be enjoyable—meant to fool the unsuspecting tourist into thinking that he or she was actually having an enjoyable time. Knowing full well that they were succumbing to this flagrant manipulation, they ate there anyway—would have missed the sea lions, otherwise.

"They're like corporate cheerleaders. Business gets top billing with the TV newscasts," complained Tracy, over a Mai Tai.

"Don't be obtuse," said Ben, sporting another boutonniere. "TV newscasts are corporations—they're all connected—the stations, the advertisers. What you see on the news is what they want you to see." He glanced over at Ashley.

"Sort of their form of solipsss…" said Tracy, struggling.

"Solipsism?" offered Steve.

"Yes, thanks, Steve," Tracy replied.

"What do you mean?" asked Ben.

"Nothing exists or is real, but the TV," Tracy stated, staring at him as if to say, "You dumbshit"!

"So, I'm finally on TV," quipped Les.

"And it's true what they say," said Ashley, "you are at least ten pounds heavier. And I don't like that make-up." But they had to keep it cool, not give the others a clue as to what was going on between them. There was the Ben factor and they didn't want to spoil the moment.

"This is what you believe, Tracy, that nothing is real, but TV?" Ben asked, hoping to score a few points.

"No, but it's what they believe."

That was a nice one, Ben noted. Nowhere to go with that one. He decided to nod and cover his mouth with Mai Tai.

"I think they should ease the rules in professional football…why not basketball too. Sure, throw that in," Les announced, suddenly realizing that that had been the booze reading his mind and leaking the information. All the TV talk had forced him to ponder the instant replay—something in there about reality.

"That one came out of left field," remarked Steve, as he sat sipping a beer.

"Wouldn't work for baseball much," Ben observed.

"Okay, sports fans, what wouldn't work for baseball?" Ashley inquired, though not absolutely intrigued at the prospect of discussing adults playing with balls.

"Loosen up the rules, not so many fouls. You know what I mean?" said Les, apparently rather interested in the topic. "Wouldn't work for baseball—not enough contact, unless the pitching. But for football and basketball, it would be fine; there would be more game time. Those players making those obscene salaries—make 'em earn it! Make the game more entertaining!"

Ashley was speechless—a rarity. Ben was considering the idea. Steve was thinking about those salaries and Tracy didn't really think that sports belonged on TV.

"Are you serious?" asked Ashley, once her wind returned. "Do you actually want to watch men pummeling each other?"

Les had seen that expression before. Was he willing to throw it all away to honesty? Somewhat honest? Mai Tai had let him down. "Are you kidding?" he said. "Of course not. Who watches that bullshit anyway." He glanced at her, hoping.

Ashley stared at him, saw that hopeful glint in his eyes, but decided to let this one pass. Filed, but forgotten. Les saw the file cabinet close.

"Shall we conclude our experiment? Before we get too drunk?" suggested Ashley.

"That sounds fine to me," said Steve. "Let's get this thing over with."

"Well, it worked," concluded Ben. "Discussion over."

"What do you mean, it worked?" insisted Tracy. "Steve is right back where he started."

"And glad to be there," Steve added.

"It did stop greedy behavior in Bateson," stated Ben.

"Okay, so our little experiment had its little effect," said Ashley, yet not so diminutively. "But we failed to stop greed successfully. If we'd have given him more, company would have folded. Been able to dose most of upper management, same thing."

"Sure, there are many factors," insisted Ben. "Many things that could have affected an outcome, but it is possible to stop greed."

"Yeah," Tracy stated, "Look what happened to that senior VP, the fancy dresser. He killed himself. That was a nice outcome."

"But we can't say that was a direct result of our experiment," defended Ben. "What about the other side of the coin. Every time this business fires a bunch of people, I'll bet there are times when one or two of them commits suicide." What a comeback, he speculated. He turned to Ashley seeking approval—it wasn't there.

"I think you nailed it, Ben," piped in Les. "There are too many factors—social, genetic, probably others—that could influence greed, or the greed gene. It is far too complicated to try to fix."

"The molecular biology is pretty straight forward," stated Ben.

"If you say so," replied Les, unconvinced. "Well, then just the social factors. Society isn't ready…"

"Society would collapse," pronounced Steve.

"We don't know what society would do," declared Ashley.

"Too many factors," concluded Tracy, waving over a waiter for another pitcher.

This conversation waned and the new Mai Tai arrived; Tracy began pouring all around. Ben placed a hand over his glass, oddly declining further spirit.

The evening progressed as they finished their seafood—having had a meal very similar to their barking buddies below. It was to be an early evening for all. Les still had to devise a plan for gaining access to Ashley's room, avoiding detection. The air smelled of espionage mixed with fish and alcohol. As they stood to depart for the Armada, Ben spoke.

"Didn't anyone notice my boutonniere?"

"Oh, it's so lovely," Steve mocked.

"It's nice," said Tracy.

Ashley was standing left of Ben. Bells were sounding in Les's mind—espionage, refusing drink, seafood; no, seafood didn't matter—the flower! All in about two small fractions of a second.

"Would you like to smell it?" Ben asked Ashley. She bent forward to get a whiff. Swiftly—before the orders came down from central nervous system control—Les reached over and turned the flower up. The spray hit Ben's nose and eyes.

"Dammit!" Ben cursed, and groped at the table for a napkin. He frantically wiped his face. "Dammit! he reiterated, finishing the mop up. "Can't a guy play a joke anymore?" This was a four tabler.

"Would have been a riot, Ben," commented Ashley, sincere in her sarcasm.

"Nice try, Ben," said Les.

*

The music was already playing when he reached her door—the bump and grind. It had been a long time with no bumpin' and grindin', he regretted. Ever since, ever since the time when he'd lost his marbles. Found 'em. He knocked, she answered.

"Gil, honey, great to see you," Dolly said, from under her hair. The white robe with the fluff covered the rest below that deep neckline. She grabbed him in her arms and he reciprocated, locking lips. They two-stepped back; Dolly managed to shut the door with part of an arm that she had strained to free.

Inside, the floor and walls were bumping with grinding cat furs. He got dizzy from the sounds, colors, and that pesky lack of oxygen that came along every time he greeted her. Gil cautiously made his way over to the chair and eased himself down. She was already suited up. Off came the robe, on came the twirl. Back on course, he mused, steady as she goes.

*

Beverly figured that a little nip and tuck might prevent any further scheming by her husband. She didn't want to suffer through anything like that last bout of ruthlessness. Bev worried that it might have given her worry wrinkles—this worry gave her worry—the cycle must be stopped! She was convinced that those wrinkle creams were a lot of bird shit. Magic creams. She'd decided to inform Gil of her upcoming surgery some time this month, when she caught him in a reasonable mood—needed a wide window.

Things had entirely returned to normality. Beverly wasn't running out back and scaring the gardener before dinner. Order and sanity had been restored to the estate. Even the gong had reacquired that peaceful, predictable gong, sounding Gil's return. The front door opened.

"Hi, honey," Bev said, as the overcoat and briefcase entered with Bateson. He suffered his face peck. "Have a nice day?" she inquired.

"Fine, fine, Bev. How was your day?" he returned, allowing the maid to partially disrobe him.

"Fine, dear, fine," she replied, resting her hands on his wrist and giving him her cranked-up-on-the-sweet smile.

"That's good, you know, I'm beat. Had a rough one today. Could you have my dinner sent up? I think I'll make it an early night," he said, freeing his wrist and patting her shoulder.

"Certainly, dear, just as you like," she responded. Her arms dropped comfortably to her sides. Bateson went upstairs with surprising speed for such an exhausted man. Her smile remained of its own accord. Beverly chirped to the maid, "And you're my bastard."

Chapter 20

Eugene Richmond was the section head. As a head in the pharmaceutical division, he could greet his underlings any damned way he pleased—within acceptable bounds, had to watch the sexual harassment, for example. But they weren't going to instruct him on appropriate intradivisional conduct, if that's what it was called. Boldness was part of his personality—maybe he was too loud at times, but this was simply part of his personality. Nowhere in his job description did it say, "Absolutely, don't be yourself!"

He was wearing tennis shoes, so he wouldn't click on the linoleum—had to watch the squeak, but that was doable. Also, anyone in the hall—he did not wish to be observed acting in a stealthful manner. Eugene managed to enter Ben's lab unseen and without a sound.

"Morning, Ben," he blasted, from about fifteen feet away.

His target, who was stooped over the lab bench filling vials, didn't flinch.

"Good morning, Gene," replied Ben, calmly, attention focused upon the vials. He'd been bathing in the luxury of the repetition—very Zen.

"I see you're hard at it. Getting things done?"

"Slow and steady," said Ben, relishing the alliteration and flow of the words, as they floated away.

This, Eugene found to be definitely contrary to company policy, but it had a nice ring to it.

"Ben, you do have some deadlines, as I'm sure you are aware," stated Eugene, grabbing those reins.

"We'll get there, Gene, we'll get there."

"Slow and steady doesn't sound like you'll be getting there any time soon." Eugene crossed his arms.

"But, Gene, we will get there," said Ben, adding the final drops to a vial, "and…just…in…time."

"Are you putting me on here, Ben? Is this some kind of joke?"

"Is what some kind of joke, Gene?"

"This coolness show. This 'I'm so cool' thing you're putting on."

Ben stopped pouring, placed his materials down on the bench, and turned to his boss.

"Come on, Gene, what should I be doing? How do you want me to act?"

"Show me some pep, some enthusiasm."

"So you want me to pretend to be overly excited about all of this, is that it, Gene?" Ben asked, smiling.

"What are you being so smug about?"

"This conversation. I am getting the job done here, Gene. I will meet my deadline."

"Well, I can't ask for anything more than that, I guess," said Eugene, still in a fog about his actions and motives. He wondered if Ben was somehow after his job.

"Are you feeling okay, Gene?"

Now he knew Ben was after his job. Pulling the old, "Boss can't seem to take the pressure," routine. I'm onto you, my friend, Gene told himself.

"I'm fine, Ben. How are you?"

"Fine as well, Gene," Ben replied, genuinely glad.

"Good then, Ben. Keep up the good work. Well, got to make the rounds, see you later," and Eugene was out the door, still concerned about Ben's plans for taking over his job.

*

It felt as if they weren't being watched. No looking over the shoulder, nothing, no strings. Les was to meet Ashley at Sea-Tac airport, mid-morning on a Tuesday. He'd called in sick for the rest of the week.

Getting off a plane was not glamorous—nothing he could do would ever be called glamorous—but unless you were in First Class (something he'd never done), it was pretty much a cattle crawl getting out of a jet. Unless you were in the first row or second of economy, but you still had to wait for First Class, and they took their sweet time. That was one of the perks of First Class, taking your damn sweet time.

So, he surmised, one could not exit a jet in an absolutely carefree mood, unless one had been in First Class and no disturbances had occurred during the entire flight. Not one disturbance, so it was therefor extremely unlikely that any person could leave an airliner in an unencumbered, happy mood.

He braced himself for the moment that Ashley came out of the gate—that sounded very cattle ranch too. He knew she wasn't the type to waste money on First Class, so she wouldn't have been there—unless she'd been able to get a free upgrade. So, there was a decent chance that Ashley would be the last one off the plane. And none too happy. She was.

No plans had been made, so they hit I-5 heading north. At 10:30 in the morning, there wasn't much traffic, but this stretch near Seattle was never a free ride. Not for the last ten years or so, Les had heard. He wasn't used to it, rarely came down this way. This car had never entered the diamond lane because Les did not know how many occupants it took to rate the diamond. No rush, anyway.

Ashley had dressed sensibly for the flight. Nothing fancy. No high heels, nylons. She'd worn jeans, shirt, and shoes. Les could not resist a woman in jeans. Didn't have to be tight, but just the fact of a woman wearing jeans. He felt an urge to be surrounded by nature. This was difficult, as nature, in this region, was on a fast sprint away—being chased by developers and disposed city councils, herding an unruly mass of commuters. Les headed toward Edmonds; he knew of a decent park.

You left your car in a lot at the top of a ravine and went down a reasonable incline for about half the trail. Meadowdale County Park was about a couple miles long and a half mile wide of riparian woodland—some old growth still standing. It was an island, surrounded on three sides by suburban residence, and the forth by Puget Sound. Once you got in, you couldn't tell the difference—until you reached the sea, there was nothing to dissuade you from imagining yourself in the middle of a huge forest. They took a hike.

Ashley remained reticent. Les was winging it. The walk and sitting on the beach did not sate his need to be encompassed by nature. When they got back to the car, he headed up Highway 99, and turned left to Mukilteo. There was a ferry terminal.

Even though your car was tagging along, a ferry ride always gave him a sense of getting away, taking a cruise. This was no Love Boat, but Les could feel something happening. Ashley still seemed something…guarded or merely impenetrable. He could not figure her out—thought that a cruise might open her up.

Once they reached the town of Clinton on Whidbey Island, Les took them up the hill onto the highway. He remained on wing mode, chanced a right onto another highway—or the same, he wasn't certain—heading north. Some stray Bed and Breakfast billboards determined their fate—for at least that night.

Ashley chose one with a room that opened onto the beach, a sliding glass window full of The Sound.

They had coffee on the sand the next morning. The rising sun warmed their right sides as they discussed a future in the distance. Still no immediate plans.

"I am tired of it, Les. It's like Steve said, I think it was Steve. We're all just hamsters on a wheel."

"Hamster wheelin'."

"I want to get out of it."

"Could be like Lemmings too."

""What?" she asked from her supine position, stretched out, legs crossed.

"Take this area, for example. It is getting more and more crowded. Road rage, sidewalk rage. Folks get more and more stressed. At some point, they have to get out."

"And the Lemming reference would involve…"

"You know, the Lemmings. Population increases, reaches a critical density, and they start a mass march to the sea. They all jump off a cliff."

"Les, I'm not planning to jump off a cliff."

"I know," he said, sitting on her left, sipping very strong coffee.

"I need something better. More quality time."

"There's a rare phrase."

She got up on her elbows—wasn't happy with anyone knocking her phrases. Even if the phrase in question was really begging to be bumped.

"Are we a…" she asked, gazing up at him.

"That's the way I feel," Les replied, holding his eyes to the north.

"Me too. So, well, we can't do this commute thing."

"Relationship?"

"I don't want a commute relationship."

"I don't either."

"I was thinking of quitting my job, moving up here with you."

"I was thinking that too. Not because…well, because I couldn't live in L.A. Even with you, not in L.A."

"I'll be happy to leave, Les."

"Good…what would you do up here? Not that you have to do…"

"I thought about that. Open up a small practice, rent a little office."

"You know how to do that?"

"Sure. We'd need a big apartment. We could even buy a house."

"They're expensive," Les said, never having considered this possibility.

"We could make it."

"It's getting more and more crowded around here."

"We'll simply have to find a safe cliff for a soft landing."

He smiled.

About the Author

Angus Wynn lives in the Northwest. This is his second novel—fun with science!

Printed in the United States
52746LVS00007B/58-63